Pack

Hazard Short Fiction

Fooling   Marilyn Duckworth

Pack of Lies

Chad Taylor

Hazard Short Fiction

HAZARD PRESS
publishers

Publication of this book has been assisted by a grant from the Literature Programme of the Q.E. II Arts Council of New Zealand.

First published 1994
Copyright © 1994 Chad Taylor

ISBN 0 - 908790 - 72 - 4

Published by Hazard Press Limited,
P.O. Box 2151, Christchurch, New Zealand
Cover photograph by Kendal Simich
Author photograph by Wayne Wilson
Production and design by ORCA Publishing Services
Printed in New Zealand by
Wyatt & Wilson Print Ltd., Christchurch

To G & F

— ONE —

My hands are all bloody. They got blood on them when I wiped my head before and with the bang on my head – whatever it was, something blunt, it was hard, Christ, I gritted my teeth – it must be bleeding. It's warm and it smells. If I turned the lights on I could see exactly how bad it is but I'm not going to turn the lights on. Not just yet. Turning them on would mean trying to stand. I can't stand yet. Christ. Not just yet.

I think I am going into shock. I think I am, I can feel it. I'm pretty sure I am. I should just stand up and click the light switch now. Now. And see the blood in the mirror and know it's mine, when the bald lightbulbs snap on above the sink. I hug my knees lying sideways on the floor, sideways in the dark, waiting. My hands are sticky and warm. The taps are still on, running down the porcelain into the drain and curling away.

I dropped the card. It was a nice card as birthday cards go. To A Girl Who Is Seven. It's lying on the floor somewhere, by the door where I dropped it. It felt light between my fingers and then slippery – sticky. To a girl who's bigger and brighter every day. Blue puppies in a basket of flowers. A Very Happy Birthday To A Girl Who Is Seven. Somewhere in the dark.

The phone receiver crackles, the woman with the sweet voice still talking, chattering away, saying the police will be there very very soon. I dropped the card. I want to stand up but I can't. I will. But not yet.

Numb. I can hardly feel my legs, I'm going all numb. There is no moon through the bare windows, the only lights are the stars. The phone receiver is saying, now can you just give me your name again?

Catrina Phillips, something-something road, something-something suburb. I've said it so many times I am starting to forget. When I was small I would whisper a new word over and over again until it stopped meaning anything. And I would say, Grandma, what does it mean? When I knew perfectly well. Over and over.

God. I'm going to throw up. I really am. I'm going to be sick. I huddle my knees to my lips and smell denim. Christ. I gritted my teeth, when it hit, something blunt it was, something hard. Now don't worry because we're sending a car, it was in the area and it's on its way now, it will be there very soon. I lost the card, though. And she says: the card?

I meant to pay for it. Intended to. I picked it out and walked to the counter but the man was busy and I went to look at some books, and it wasn't until I was leaving that I realised the card was still in my hand. I stood at the front of the shop in the light of the electric eye with the doors waiting to close. If I went back inside and told them they wouldn't believe me. If I put it in my pocket and kept on walking I would be stealing it. I couldn't go either way. When I got home I wrote twenty on it. To A Girl Who's Twenty Seven.

We used to hop in front of the electric eye and watch the doors open and close.

I want my head to be alright. I hate anything when peoples' heads get hurt. Your brain is so soft, it can't take very much. You hear about kids who fall off their bike and that's it: dead. And then you hear things like the man who lived after getting a steel bar through his head. He was a steel worker, this Englishman, and it was on a building site. Someone dropped a bar – a pike – about four feet long and it fell down two stories and went through the front half of his brain. He didn't even pass out. The skin grew over and he lived for another 10 years. But then at the end of his life he went quite crazy. I guess he just lost too many brain cells in the end. The thing with head injuries is that you never know. I want someone to get here so I can find out if I am going to be okay. I want to stand up and turn the lights on. But not just yet.

The doctors don't know either. They find everything out by accident or because they are crazy themselves. One was a doctor who had his head cut open during the French Revolution. He bandaged it with a splint so it stayed open and never healed, and for the next four years he took samples of his own brain fluid. He did it by tying bits of sponge onto string and pulling them around the inside of his skull. He finally died when a knot in the string cut into the sac around his brain. That was the only thing that stopped him – he would have carried on dredging his head with a sponge forever, otherwise. That's a man of science for you – that's what medicine is. The only thing that stops them is dying, and when they die someone else wants to cut them up. Like they cut up murderers and prisoners for autopsies and medical schools. I mean, if they base all their research on what they cut out of insane people then how do they learn to treat normal people. They can't even treat old people. Old people get sat in a corner with dribble coming out of their mouth and they can't even speak. They piss into a tube and they die, they're vegetables. All they can do is sit and look, stare out the window until they fall apart. Stare and wait for someone to come.

The curtains are pulled back and it's late and it's dark. The stars look thicker in the smog. And my head hurts, my mind aches and it's not fair. I bite my lip. The phone receiver is still talking. Talking and talking. And the traffic is going past. Even at this time of night it is the rush hour. My hair is starting to stick to the carpet. I pull myself closer against the corner of the wall, the damp edges of wallpaper and the skirting board speckled with fly dirt. The flat is so dirty. I should clean it really. You should always have it clean. You never know when someone is going to come round. Be on your best. And I would be, but my head hurts. I must have gritted my teeth and fallen down and covered my face with my hands. I don't even know. But they will tell me later. They will sort it out.

The water is running over the edge of the sink and seeping into the carpet. I can feel it creep under my head and shoulders, toward the telephone. It will be dangerous if it touches. A shock from the phone will kill you straight. When they first invented telephones it happened all the time. Women picked up the receiver wearing heavy gold earrings and the electricity jumped right out.

I have been in this flat forever, lying here, sitting in the dark, making cups of tea, ringing people up. There are a whole bunch of people I need to call but I'm not going to get round to it, I'm not going to get it done. I've got to clean first, do my hair, get tidied up. I bought this hat, a red straw hat. From a secondhand place. Fuck it won't even fit on my head now. It won't even go on. My ears are ringing and the phone is off the hook.

When the police lights arrive they make a lonely noise, tyres crunching on the empty driveway. I listen to the footsteps looking to see which flat it is and the radio and the inevitable knock on the door – if I could open the door it would already be open. Wouldn't it? They can't work that out.

They look through the window and they look back through the curtains. Please hurry. Really. Break a window. I don't mind. It belongs to the landlord anyway. So. Each person casts a dozen different shadows, overlapping.

I roll on my back, still holding my knees to my chest and call out: break the window. The shadows stiffen. PLEASE BREAK THE FUCKING WINDOW. I'm not going to yell help. They rattle the

10

lock. Fuck, fuck, fuck. It's on a chain. IT'S ON A CHAIN. You think they could work it out. THE DOOR'S ON A FUCKING CHAIN. What do they want, a key under the mat? I can't get up to unlock the door. I don't want to try and stand just yet. PLEASE BREAK – fuck it. Alright. HELP. Alright? Loud enough?

The door jumps off its hinges like it's been trained and the glass goes everywhere and then they are on me. They turn me over and examine my head and someone is calling for an ambulance, a stretcher, a doctor. They find a first aid kit and press cotton wool on my head. They wrap me in a blanket and say to keep still, but I'm not moving, I'm not going to try and stand up just yet. I want to stay where I am, curled up on the floor under the rug, in a warm corner with my head in my hands, where I got hit in my hands, where it hurt. I want someone to stroke my head. The policewoman says she will stroke my head. She puts rubber gloves on first.

— *TWO* —

Traffic is passing on the road outside. All the nurses and patients and people visiting. There is a Bambina parked over by the trees. I used to drive one. I remember when I brought it I came in and everyone asked what I'd chosen and I said an Italian car, because the Italians were the best at Formula One racing.

When the Italians first started developing Formula One racing cars they made them small, like they made all their other cars. Fiat made most of them. Anyway, there was nothing wrong with the small cars mechanically or design-wise – in fact many of them were as fast as the other competitors. But the Italian team never won any races. They couldn't figure it out. They put the cars through tests and trial runs and they took the engines apart and put them back together again, but no one could find anything wrong with them. So the Fiat bosses flew in a German analyst and he went through their whole technique – design, construction, maintenance, everything. And the German guy realised what was wrong. The problem, see, wasn't the car at all – it was the driver. The Italians were really upset when he said it because that's like the most insulting thing you can say to an Italian man – that he can't drive. But when everyone had calmed down the German analyst explained: it's not that the drivers aren't good – it's just that they're *too big*.

The trick with racing car driving is that when he's the right size, the driver becomes the car's centre of gravity. A Formula One car is designed so that every time you take a corner the four wheels skid *around* the driver, like a top. If the driver is too big then everything goes out of whack and the car doesn't skid evenly. The front wheels skid a little more or the back wheels don't skid enough and you come out of the curve on the wrong angle. And then, once you're on the wrong angle, you lose your acceleration. When you jump the pedal the car doesn't go forward, it goes sideways. And that's where all your gas goes. You're slower on the track, you use more gas, you eat up the tyres, and you have to go into the pit stops more often. And that was why the Italians were losing races.

After the Italians thought about it, they paid the German analyst a whole lot of money and sent him home, and then they started looking for drivers who were the right size. In fact they didn't even care if they found people who were drivers – they just wanted someone the right height and weight, which, for the sort of cars they were making then, was around five foot. The racing team had posters printed and put up in every village in Italy, and they went on the radio, and Mussolini made speeches about it, and it became a sort of national search. They didn't want boys, of course, because boys can grow bigger. They only wanted short men.

They tested a lot of the men who applied, hundreds if not thousands, and they took a lot of them on the team, but the most famous of them was a man called Guiseppe Marchetti who stood four foot nine. The racing team chose him straight away because he was perfect – the right height, and he used to work as a taxi driver, which meant that he was pretty fast.

So this guy Marchetti became the world's shortest Formula One racer. All the other guys from the other teams laughed at him when he walked into the pits because he was tiny – the English driver was five eleven and the Germans were pretty big too. All the other teams were racing big cars at that time and so hadn't noticed the thing about the driver's weight much. I guess once a car gets over a certain weight it doesn't matter if the driver is big or small. Certainly the Italians were the first ones to notice the anomaly.

Anyway, on his first race Marchetti just shot through and nobody could believe it. The race was held in the south of France and everyone was cheering like crazy for the French Renault driver, who stood five foot eight, but Marchetti passed him as if he was standing still and his Fiat engine was screaming because it was burning around so fast. After he crossed the finish line the engine actually started to catch fire but that didn't matter, he had won the race and he became the first Italian for years and years to do so. The crowd hoisted him up on their shoulders and carried him to the presentation stand. The mayor gave a speech but no one could hear it over the shouting, and then they asked Marchetti to say something but the microphone stand wouldn't fold down that far so he refused because he wouldn't be made fun of. Two big blonde women presented him with the trophy which was as tall as he was and after he took it the women lifted him up with one arm each, so his feet were dangling off the ground, and everyone was cheering and cheering.

Marchetti became like the best driver in Italy. He was the fastest and Fiat were making him the best engines they could, and they not only kept the Italian cars small but actually designed them around his body. They took plaster casts of him in the driver's seat and weighted them, for accuracy. The plaster casts sell for hundreds of thousands of dollars today – or lire, I guess, depending on whatever the exchange rate is.

He won all the Formula One races for six years, plus racing in a lot of other categories as well and winning them, and the Italian team became the most famous team, and Mussolini gave him a couple of medals. It was like a joke at the time: every year Marchetti would win the Formula One, every year he would get another medal from Mussolini. He was a millionaire and as famous as a movie star. He married this incredibly beautiful fashion model and she lived in a big house, but he went and raced all the time, and still spent hours and hours with the mechanics, helping design the racing cars and stuff. I don't know if she minded that too much, but she wasn't perfectly happy with it.

Anyway. The other teams who raced in the Formula One were getting really frustrated with not winning, especially the Germans. Hitler had a whole lot of money in Formula One racing because he wanted the Germans to beat the world at everything, probably as practice for both sides before the war – so Germany could practise winning and everyone else could practise looking up to them, I guess, that was how Hitler thought. So the Mercedes team especially wanted to start winning motor races. They did all this research into the Italian cars but couldn't come up with any answers until one day someone heard about the German analyst who had gone down and done work for the Italian team, and they called him up and arranged a meeting, and he told them the secret was the driver's weight and size, and suddenly everything clicked.

That was in 1935 and for the next five years leading up to the Second World War, the Italians never won another Formula One race in that time. The Germans trained up drivers that were the right shape and size for their bigger, more powerful cars and beat everyone flat. Marchetti just about went crazy. And the Italian team started designing bigger cars, the same size as the Mercedes and the Porsches, and looking therefore for bigger drivers, and suddenly Marchetti was going out of a job. They fired him in 1938 in favour of some other guy who was over six foot.

After the Italians dropped him, Marchetti said he was going to enter as a private competitor, but he couldn't find a sponsor. So he paid for everything himself and the cost was fantastic. He started drawing up designs for a new racing car – for street racing, because he could see that that was where the future of racing was. He designed it around his own body weight and height, because he still believed that a really good small car could go faster than a big one. But it was costing him a fortune to develop. He started by selling off his properties and his tools and even some of his trophies. In the end his wife left him and he couldn't keep up the payments to his mechanic and he went bankrupt – this was in 1939. He went back to driving a taxi in Rome. He drove really fast to get lots of fares but even that wasn't enough – the banks were going to put him in jail. So he sold the designs for his new car to Fiat, in May 1939. He was killed in the war, I read, but I think he killed himself really, because he had come so far and tasted what it was to be really great, and now he had nothing again, and he couldn't handle it.

Fiat just put the designs away and forgot about them. They only bought them to be kind to Marchetti, I think they felt they owed him. But in the sixties someone dusted off the designs and changed them a little bit here and there and started making them as a normal car, and that became the Bambina. It was perfect because it was so small, and everyone bought it for driving around cities in. But whoever took out the plans remembered Marchetti because they left his name on the car: just under the lid, the bonnet, when you lift it up, the word MARCHETTI has been stamped into the frame – no explanation or number or anything, nothing but the word caked in grime from the engine. Most people who buy Bambinas now wouldn't even know it's there, let alone what it means.

— *THREE* —

'Catrina?' He holds out the card, puts it in my lap. 'Think this is yours.'

To A Girl Who Is Twenty-Seven. Yes.

'Your birthday, is it?'

No, my friend's. Babe's.

'How's the head feeling?'

Fine.

'Bill Howard. Do you remember, we…'

Yes. Not that I do really. All cops look the same.

'At the flat, that's right.' He holds his ID close so I can see without having to lean forward. He folds it back in the flap of his wallet and puts it in his breast pocket. Brown tweed and curly hair and big thick shoes. He sniffs. 'The nurses said you're a little tired. But I thought I'd come in and see how you were.'

The iron leg of the chair squeaks as he pulls it up. He holds his left fist in his right hand on the edge of the bed. He has big hands.

'Do you work with Babe?'

No. She works at the tenants' society. Our birthday's in the same month. But she looks older than me. Because she's taller. It was her party last night. I didn't have time to look for presents. I only got her the card. I turn it in my hand.

'Twenty-seven,' he says.

Yeah. They don't print cards with Happy 27th on them, though. I don't suppose women want to know. I guess it's different for guys.

He smiles. 'Not much different.'

Well.

'That was at the Astor…?'

17

Yeah. The Astor is sort of the student pub. Everyone goes there.

'Can I ask you some questions, Catrina?'

I don't know if I feel like it.

'Well, I've read your statement and there are some details I want to go over with you. I'd like to get some facts clear in my head, build up a picture. You know?'

I guess.

'Good. Now you haven't identified the person who attacked you…'

No.

'Did you see the person at all?'

No.

'Was there anyone outside the flat before you went in?'

No.

'You didn't see anyone?'

No.

'And no one followed you home?'

No.

'You were coming from university?'

Yes.

He nods. 'University. It's hard to get in these days. My daughter's finding that.'

I guess.

'What course are you doing?'

What do you want to know for?

'Just interested.' He smiles again. 'You don't have to tell me if you don't want to.'

The fluorescents are still burning, white lines reflected in the wide, red windows as the sun begins to rise.

Political studies.

He nods. 'I'd like to do something like that sometime. Later, maybe, adult education, something like that. When do you graduate?'

Well, I've got, shit, I have to count... a few more units in all. It always seems like there's a few more.

'Okay.' He opens his notebook. 'I have some statements here... We had a report...'

A police report?

'No, witness reports... some people who say they saw you in the early evening, in the Ascot. They say you were having a drink with some other students, friends of yours. And you stayed for...' He flicks through the pages. 'Four or five rounds...?'

There were a lot of people drinking. Birthdays, you know.

'Of course. Drink much?'

No.

'One of our people spoke to someone who said that you were in a distressed state. The person says you were in the toilets – crying, is what they said.'

I don't think so.

'Are you sure?'

The truth is I was a little pissed off yesterday. I'd had a full day and I'd had to carry my books, and my back was sore. It all kind of builds up. All the little things do. It gets you down a bit.

He reaches into his jacket for a thick, dry fold of papers and spreads them flat on the sheet. 'I understand. So that's what you think this person saw?'

I guess so. I mean, I'm not that person, but it sounds like that to me.

'Okay.' He gives me a different look. Just a brief glance, as if he is having a new thought and there is a new problem. But that is only for a moment and afterward he returns to the papers, which are neatly typed.

'We looked at the report on your injuries, and as you know we looked around the flat...' He flicks through the pages. 'You had concussion. Swelling and bleeding around the side of the head...' he stabs fat fingers at his temple, '...which implies being struck with a pointed object. Now, the front door of your flat opens onto a polished wooden landing...' the fat fingers make themselves into a little corridor, '...which leads to a kitchenette. In the kitchenette is a stove. The corner of that stove is bloodied.' The fat fingers hang in mid-air. 'Do you remember falling on the stove, Catrina?'

Falling? No.

'Were you pushed against the stove?'

I don't know. My eyes itch. Maybe I was. I think... I rub my nose with my unbandaged hand. I think maybe I could have been.

'How do you think that might have happened?'

I guess... whoever it was... gave me a shove. Hit me on the side of the head and I tried to stand up, to stay straight but I slipped.

'Slipped?'

My head's starting to hurt again.

'You're a very lucky girl.'

I don't fucking feel like it.

'Please Catrina. I'm not here to upset you.'

You fucking are. You fucking are upsetting me.

'Please calm down.'

I am fucking calmed down. I sit back and push the air out of the pillows and fold my arms and he waits, staring.

'Can you remember...'

Why don't you go fuck yourself.

He takes a breath.

I sit still.

He stares and waits but I keep my mouth shut.

He lets out his breath.

'Okay.'

He sits back again.

'I have arguments like this with my daughter,' he smiles.

I bet.

'Catrina, do you know someone called Wayne Martin?'

What?

'Wayne Martin.' He flicks out a photo that doesn't look like him at all. 'Young guy, about 25 years old.'

I'm not...

'Catrina. This isn't helping anyone. Please be honest now. Do you know Wayne Martin?'

Yes. A long time ago. Before Babe.

'You go out with him?'

Not now.

'But you used to?'

Yes.

'How are things between him and you, now?'

We're... I look for the word. You can never phrase it when you want. Friends. We're friends, I guess.

'Good friends?'

Um. Sort of.

'Catrina, about five minutes after you called in last night, one of our cars picked up Wayne Martin.'

Oh.

'Right in your neighbourhood, about two blocks away from your flat. Drunk. Now, that's not a coincidence, is it?'

What happened?

'He's helping us with our enquiries.'

Oh.

'Did he push you into the stove, Catrina? Across the floor?'

I don't remember.

'Could he have borrowed a spare key from you?'

I don't recall.

'Please try.'

I am.

'Catrina, this is hard for you to say, I realise that. You went out with him for a long time, didn't you? We understand the…' He reaches for the word. '…*conflict*. The problems. Conflict of interest. We don't *blame* you for that. You're not the one in trouble here. Wayne is the one in trouble. We've got him. We had him even before you were admitted to hospital. One block away from the reported incident, intoxicated. Drunk and aggressive. We *knew* what had happened. *I* knew. But when *these* came in…' he shakes the witness reports, 'there were some bad things said about our procedure…'

I don't have anything against the police.

'I know you don't. I know that. And there were things said about you. The sort of things that upset you – but relax. Alright? That's what I'm here to tell you. I know now – we know – that's not the case.

'So. Just tell me now, very quietly. Just between you and me.' Big hairy jacket. 'No details, just what happened. Very simply. We can follow up the rest later. Did you argue? Were you seeing someone? He's a violent bloke…' Moles on his hands, scratches. 'You argued about… something? Were you drinking with him this evening? Did he invite himself round? You let him in, had a beer, few drinks, had an argument, something like that? Is that what happened? It looks that way to us.'

Yellow fingernails, smoker. First knuckles of his fingers smell.

'Did you argue,' he shrugs, 'on the way home…?'

I hold the pillow.

'All we need's a yes, Catrina.' He smiles. 'And we can deal with the rest.'

He'd go to jail.

'With his record? Yes, he would.' He taps the blank page with his pen. 'You'd be quite safe.'

He smiles. My head hurts. I try to say things but my head hurts. When he smiles his lips disappear beneath his moustache.

'You know, my girl's about as old as you.'

Hugging the pillow.

'My daughter. She's about your age.'

That's weird. What would it be like having a cop as a father? I think you would need a sister. One at least.

'We have enough to lay charges…'

I'm feeling so tired.

'Perhaps we could come and see you this afternoon. Or you could come into the station. For a fuller statement.'

The nurse said I wasn't allowed to get tired. I remember she said so.

'It's important we can act on this, Catrina. There's a lot of…'

Can you get the nurse to come in please? I'd like you to get the nurse to come in. I think I'm having a relapse or something.

His smile disappears.

'Alright.'

Can you get her now, please?

'Where do you think you'll be staying, Catrina?'

Could you get the nurse?

'Where, Catrina?'

With Babe.

'I'll give you a call.'

I don't remember her number.

'Is it listed?'

I'm not sure. I think I've got temporary amnesia or something. Can you just get the nurse?

Through the window the sun is slowly rising above the trees and the kitchen people are starting to wheel in breakfast on wobbly trolleys. Officer Howard turns and walks out, his big shoes squeaking on the linoleum.

I didn't want to piss him off too much. He had big hands and big arms. I bet he could lift you right off the ground if he wanted. I stand the birthday card next to the bed, so I can see it from where I lie.

— *FOUR* —

Babe has always been difficult about her birthday and now that she is having more of them it seems to be getting more difficult. I tried to talk her into the idea early because I figured the problem would only exacerbate itself but she said no, she still didn't feel like having a big fuss made over her on the day. I remember one time I invited her for a picnic on Mt Eden. She was really cagey about it. Finally she said she'd come if she could bring a friend and I said okay. I baked her a chocolate cake and bought champagne and remembered to bring the cutlery and a blanket and glasses wrapped in tea-towels. We arranged to meet on the summit around midday.

I was still waiting for her at 12:30. It was the middle of summer and really hot and my arms were aching holding the hamper, but I figured she would show. At one o'clock I decided to go looking. It didn't take long to find her. She was down the side of the hill under the trees with her friend. In the shade. I just climbed back up to the top of the hill.

There were people riding horses around the hill, taking them up the slow road and then letting them climb down the rougher parts of the slope. There is a riding club around Mt Eden somewhere. My aunt rides there. She has ridden ever since she was a little girl.

She was brought up on a farm someplace and she and all her friends had horses, like children have bikes now, and they rode everywhere: to school and to visit each other and to go into town. One day my aunt's friend told her about a woman who read palms and they decided to go and see her. The palm-reader was about eighty and living by herself and she wouldn't read palms for money – she'd do it if you took her a packet of biscuits or some tea or

25

something like that. She didn't like making money off it.

So my aunt and her friend, who was called Pip, rode over to the other side of the valley to meet this palm-reader. There were no proper roads then, only dirt tracks across the fields, and the ride took a couple of hours, which is a long time on horseback. When they got there the woman took them inside and sat them down and they gave her a packet of biscuits and a chocolate bar and they had tea together, and talked about nothing in particular. Pip and my aunt were really careful not to say anything which would give them away.

The woman did my aunt first. She spread my aunt's right hand out on the table and ran her fingertips along the lines and said, well, you live on a farm, and you've done this and this, and it all turned out to be true. Then she turned to my aunt's left hand and said you'll grow up in the city, and you'll marry a man who looks like such and such, but you won't stay together very long... and things like that. My aunt was very excited by it and a lot of the things since then have turned out to be true, they've happened, although she doesn't talk about the day very much.

When it was Pip's turn the woman read her right hand and got some things right although there were a few things wrong, but that was okay and Pip was really excited. Then when the woman turned to Pip's left hand she went quiet. She said nothing, only stared. And Pip said, what is it? And the woman said, I'll tell your fortune but not out loud, I'll write it down for you, and you mustn't read it here, you must read it when you get home. Pip got very excited. The woman wrote it down on a piece of notepaper and folded it and gave it to my aunt to carry saying, you mustn't give it to her until I've said. The girls left saying thank you, and mounted up and started riding.

It was getting towards the end of the day and they were both in a hurry to get home anyway, let alone to read the note and find out what the secret was, and they were excited as hell. After talking about it they decided 'home' meant anywhere on Pip's property so it would be safe to read it as soon as they reached the outskirts of the farm. They started the horses up to a gallop and headed back. They were about two miles away from the farm when Pip's horse caught its hoof in a ditch and threw her and cracked her head open on the hard summer ground. She was killed instantly.

My aunt rode back to the farm and got everyone and they came driving and riding and running out to where Pip lay but she was stone dead, of course, there was nothing they could do. They took my aunt home and she went into her room and lay on the bed. And then she remembered the palm-reader's note, much much later, and she took it out of her shirt and opened it up and it said, 'no future.'

I always wondered how the palm-reader felt when she read that. She must have known what was going to happen, if not specifically then in a general way, she must have figured it out. My aunt never said if she went back to the palm reader. She only told me that story once, after she'd had a bit to drink, and when I asked her about it again she didn't really go into the details.

I watched the horses on the side of the hill for a long time and waited for Babe and her friend to turn up. When they did show I promised I hadn't been waiting long. I looked at her and her friend drinking champagne and giggling and wondered what would happen next, if it would last until the following birthday or what. We lit the candles on the cake and watched them burn in the open air.

— FIVE —

The buzzer rings muffled from the other end of the hall. My head throbs under my hat. Babe's house has not been painted in a long time and if you touch the weatherboards what colour remains peels off in parchment flakes. Wasps hang above the weeds. The garden here used to really be something. Whoever owned the house before grew the front trees into animal shapes – one was a duck and another was a dog. The back lawn was concreted over and everything in it was made out of cement – flowers and fountains and gnomes and seals and pelicans. Babe was very proud of it. The tree-animals have pretty much lost their shape, now.

Babe opens the door in her kimono and blinks and doesn't say anything. I hold out the card. She looks at it, and then at me, and then takes the card and opens it with one hand against her breast and reads it slowly. She combs the hair back behind her ears with the card tip and folds her arms and leans on the door. She knew what it said anyway.

'Well,' she murmurs.

Didn't mean to get you out of bed.

'Wasn't even sleeping.'

I left without giving it to you. I thought you should have it.

'Thank you.'

I just came round. I thought you'd be having breakfast or something. The concrete steps are dirty. It is after ten.

'Well, you'd better come in, then.'

Sorry.

'S'okay.' She leads us down the hall, leaving me to shut the door. 'You had breakfast?'

Yeah.

She stands the card on the stove top and rubs her eyes and gives me a pink stare. 'Bet you haven't.'

I'm not hungry.

'That's not what I asked you.'

I know.

She goes through the fridge. The saucepans hang on black steel hooks and garlic is on a string and the shelves are full of food. She always said she wanted a great kitchen and now she has it. She squints to read the carton label. 'Juice?'

What sort?

'Orange.'

Yes please.

'And breakfast?' She bends over the fridge again. 'You want cereal or shall I cook you something?' She takes eggs out of the tray. 'We've got bread.' She shuffles round in the cupboards. 'I bought it fresh. I'll cook you something.'

You don't need to.

'I don't mind.' She smiles. I watch the rug on the lounge floor while she cracks the eggs in a black iron pan. 'I was worried after you left.'

You don't have to worry.

'You want bacon?'

No thanks.

'Kidneys?'

Oh Jesus.

'You need some iron. You're getting anaemic.' She presses her thumb into my cheek. 'Look at that.'

Well I don't feel so good.

'Don't you?'

Is Brian up?

'At work already.' She wipes her nose. 'Toast. Yes?'

Babe.

'Yup…'

Babe?

'What?'

Babe, I'm…

'You're what?'

There's been some trouble.

'Where?'

Just something. It happened and…

'What d'you mean?'

She straightens up. I try to tell her but I can't.

'What sort of trouble?'

I wiggle behind the bench and wave my hands and stammer. I can't say it. I can't even begin. It's like trying to explain everything right from the beginning, all at once with no space for breath. You can't just explain one single thing. And that's why explaining is always a waste of time, always. I just take off my hat and it's there, under the straw.

'Oh my God. God, Trina. Trina? What happened?'

It takes me ages to talk.

'Trina? Shit. Jesus. What hit you? Who was it? Jesus.' She stares at the bloody bandage. 'Christ it's a mess. It's slipped.' She starts tucking it back in place. 'Jesus, Trina. Have you reported it? What…'

I spoke to the police.

'What happened?'

They said it's some guy, they've got some leads. And. I guess. And. That's…

'Oh honey.'

She asks me a whole lot of questions I can't answer and I start blubbering again so she stops and says, look, you can tell me after breakfast. I stand there looking stupid. I don't know whether to sit down or stand up. She leans across the counter and hugs me and I knock over my juice but it doesn't matter, neither of us go to wipe it up. I just lean with my face in her big shoulders. The orange juice runs off the bench. We hug for a long time.

*

I drink my coffee outside, with the animals. There are all kinds in the backyard. There is a seal and two big cats, and some penguins and a flamingo. They are so well made, cast in moulds. The moulds are worth a lot of money now, if you can find them. They used to be made at this factory in America, down in Texas. In the wide open plains. They had the patent for cement flamingoes and they cornered the market. When lounge decoration stopped being fashionable they turned bankrupt, and nobody knows what happened to the moulds. And now cement flamingoes are in fashion again, in some circles at least. Babe is going to tear the cement up soon and plant a real garden. But she has to keep the flamingo, I tell her, picking at its pink enamel, so her kids can ride on it. 'That's a good idea.' She takes up the greasy dish. 'More toast?'

No. I ate like a pig. Thank you.

She cleans up everything. I stretch out on the sun chair. The swing-frame squeaks when she sits down with fresh coffee and puts my head in her lap. The sky is flat and white. I remember this morning's sunrise, the light over the trees I saw from the hospital.

'Up on the hill,' Babe says. 'It's nice up there.' She strokes my hair. 'How're you feeling?'

That's what everyone asks.

'Well you can tell me.'

I don't feel like talking. I have kind of talked things out in my own mind. Breakfast was nice.

'Is there anything else you want?'

No.

'I want to change this dressing.'

The doctors said to keep it on.

'Just the outer bandage. It'll look nicer and you'll feel better.'

Okay. She frowns looking down on me as she changes it. I press my finger on her forehead, between her eyes. She is going to get an old lady's forehead if she is not careful. You should rest more. We should go away. Do you want to go away? I'd like to. Just for a few days.

'Wish I could.'

If you wanted. I know this place. It's such a great place. It's terrific. We could stay a few nights there.

'Nice dream.'

It's not a dream. We could do it.

She gives me her patient smile. 'You did get a bang. Easy,' she says. 'Take it easy.'

But I can't stop. It just comes out. My face is a big red mess. I messed it up by getting hurt. With this, my head. Throbbing under the bandage. I didn't mean to get hurt. It was going to be a big surprise. We had it all organised, all of us. Everyone. It's going to be a big party and we were meant to be on our way this morning. I was meant to get you to go last night, that was the whole idea. We booked at this hotel. I'm the one who's meant to get you up there but all I do is start an argument and get put in hospital and fuck it all up. We booked ahead so we could all have a weekend there, just have some fun someplace for a couple of days, get pissed and muck around and say Happy Birthday Babe – it was going to be a big surprise.

For a girl who's twenty-seven.

She looks at me with her mouth open.

'Oh baby.'

She puts both hands on my shoulders.

'Oh Trina. That's so…' She gives me a hug. 'Oh wow.' She has a smile as wide as a street. 'That's so amazing. You're wonderful. You haven't messed it… oh Trina. Oh wow.'

I've ruined it, messed everything up, I've made a wreck of it. We're supposed to be driving down. We're supposed to be *there* by now.

'You haven't, you haven't, you haven't.'

I was supposed to be the one to get you down there and it wasn't like that would be hard, all I had to say was let's go away for the weekend and that would be it, I'd ask you last week and you'd say yes and everyone else'd do the rest. But I haven't had the chance to do anything. I left it all too late and then we start scrapping. And now I'm gonna have to ring everyone and say it's off and they'll be all organised to go but it'll be fucked, a write-off.

'Oh Trina. Don't ring anyone. Don't do a thing.'

Shit.

'Listen…'

I've fucked it up.

'Listen, Trina, listen – we'll go. We'll go and we won't say anything. I'm sorry. We'll go. We've got to go. You've got to. Trina!'

Only if you want, if you really really want.

'Oh wow. Of course I want to…'

She holds me by the shoulders and says, Catrina, *you've got to*. And she squeezes my hand, puts her fingers through mine and squeezes and hugs and lies laughing, stretched out in the grass at my feet.

— *SIX* —

Where the motorway ends the traffic slows and bunches up at the first set of lights before the open road. The intersection runs between dry fields and vegetable stalls hidden under green canvas. Babe leans on the wheel. 'Jesus my stomach,' she says. 'Full of rocks.' We creep forward when the lights turn red. At least it's sunny. Everyone's getting out of town for the weekend. 'Good thing you booked, huh?' Babe gives me a smile. 'You're so sweet.' Cradles her belly. 'Shit.' After the lights she pulls over by the vegetable stalls and cuts the engine. 'One of them must have a bathroom…' She throws me the keys and gets out and walks over toward the caravans.

I lean back and watch the trucks go by.

★

After a while she comes back with white plastic shopping bags stretched with the weight of things for dessert, things to eat on the way, things that were incredibly cheap – paw-paws and soft avocados and bananas. I offer to drive but she promises she's okay, and she does look better. She shuts the fruit in the back and gets in, pushes her hair back behind her ear and rattles the column-shift. 'It takes a bit of getting used to,' she mutters. The petrol gauge says empty 'but ignore it. The whole thing's crap.' Babe scratches the windscreen. 'It didn't get a warrant. That's the pins – three hundred dollars. I mean where am I supposed to find that? I could've killed the guy.' So I spit on my finger and rub the ballpoint date out and turn the 10 into a 20 with a little work. It's a start anyway. She laughs. The traffic is moving pretty fast. She takes the birthday card off the dash and reads it while she steers.

'So when did you organise all this?'

Ages and ages ago. Everyone was talking about your birthday, doing something special. For the oldest.

'Was it your idea?'

It just sort of came up.

'I've never had a surprise party before. Are they gonna jump us when we get there, are they waiting?' She glances in the mirror. 'We might pass them going down.'

Yeah. You say if you start getting a headache.

'I'll be fine. I should be worrying about you.'

You've worried.

'And I'm the only one, it seems. Didn't the police ask anything?'

They asked about Wayne.

'That loser?'

They found his name in some file.

'He's a blot on your copybook, that guy.'

He wasn't so bad.

'He hit me once.'

What? Jesus.

'At one of the first parties you had there. We were talking and he just flared up. Sulky little bastard.' She looks in the mirror. 'At the big party. You had your new dress. We sat on the bed and read magazines. Do you remember? And just before the party ended I got up and went to the bathroom. There were only a few people left. Wayne and his mates were blocking the way to the bathroom. They wouldn't let me through. So I swore at them and they folded, of course – they fold when someone really stands up to them. But when I came out Wayne was there and he did his nut. Thoroughly. And he pushed me against the wall, with his fist. Stupid bastard. He went to hit me and I shouted and one of the others stopped him.' She strokes my cheeks. 'And then I came back to you.' She shakes her head. 'He took you for shit.'

It was Babe who told me fuck him, you've got to go. And she said it really urgently, like there was a fire or something: *You've got to.* She held me and she promised, rocked me back and forth in the taxi back seat and when I started to count how many weeks' rent I had on my fingers, she locked her fingers through mine in a fist so instead of five fingers I had ten – she was going to pay half. What'd he say? she asked. Did he throw a shit?

She lent me her suitcase so I could pack my clothes, and when I got to the flat she gave me her study lamp. She came in holding it and said, You mustn't get behind. Which was like a joke because I was so far behind already, I'd done no work all year.

She wrote out all her notes for me in shorthand and made me cram nights – we sat on the bed and she pinched me every time I made a mistake. I ended up with C passes and Babe called it the luckiest day in my life. She told me to get straight to university, where they had internal assessment and course-work evaluation and a whole lot of other things your harder-working best friend could help you with, as well as a cafeteria you could sit in all day. And that sounded wonderful, that sounded like perfection.

We used to sunbathe in her back yard. She took everything off and sat under the lawn umbrella and wondered aloud if the sun would fade her tattoo. She has a great tattoo, an ankh – on her tailbone. The artist who did it liked her so much he said I'll throw in a nipple for free so she got her tit-ring done. I didn't have anything on my body. When I joined her in the sun the neighbours complained, as if we had exceeded our nudist quota or something. The grass was clean and cut short. The squared blades left a pattern on your skin when you rolled over.

In the kitchen we ate old sausage rolls and meat pies and white bread rolls with marmalade and flat beer. We watched TV in the lounge and left grass stains on the carpet. We de-stocked the grog cupboard and worked our way through the cocktail guide.

Her bedroom was upstairs. In the last hours of the day sunlight fell across the grammar homework pinned up on the wall: lists of *Learn By Monday* and *Memorise*! She kept Polaroids filed under the glass top of her dresser and shoes on a white wire rack at the bottom of her wardrobe. I remember lying on the quilt with my chin in my hands while she tickled my back, and I would envy her winklepickers. My clothes were such a mess. I swapped: her gold slingbacks for my denim jacket, her bustier for my Docs.

Babe had lots of looks but gradually she got stuck in the sixties, with hairspray and long dresses and fingernails and eyeliner. She became a more intense version of women who demonstrate whiteware products on television, taller with longer, darker hair and tighter wool suits and pointier shoes. I didn't have any money to buy clothes then. It was the first time I'd admitted it to anyone. Babe felt sorry for me and took me out shoplifting.

She talked me into it. She borrowed my big overcoat and made me wear her raincoat even though it hadn't rained all day and we went into Woolworths and she said okay, what's something you like and I said I'd changed my mind again, I didn't want to do it. She said, go ahead, but I was getting sweaty and my hands were shaking and I was too nervous so she said okay, well, get us some pick and mix then, and then she wandered off. I started to bag sweets when one of the staff came up to me and I jumped about a mile but all he said was, please use the scoops provided and not your hands, and I smiled and said sorry and he said that's okay. I finished and paid for the sweets, counted the change out loud. Babe wasn't around so

37

I went outside holding the docket in front of me, and waited on the street and she came out a little later and said well, let's go home then. I offered her the sweets but she said not now – she kept her hands in her pockets. We walked to the bus stop around the corner and as we got behind the building she stopped and opened her coat and an electric frypan fell out. In its box. And she had stockings and T-shirts and socks and some men's business shirts and some perfume. We ate the pick and mix at night, in bed. We got zits in the morning, and squeezed them for each other. And then she would do my makeup. She did it every morning for a year.

She plucked my eyebrows and gave me cats' eyes, rouged my cheeks, powdered my nose, made my mouth go from big and red to small and black, drew lines on my face, made me grow my eyebrows back, rimmed my mouth with lip-liner, ran around my eye with pencils, pierced my ears, shaved the sides of my head, shaved my neck, plaited my hair when it grew back, gave me dreadlocks and dyed them from red to black to blonde to three-day-old-vomit yellow. And the said part never washed out or sat flat or returned to its natural skin colour. Once she drew all over me with a mapping pen and I nearly fainted in the shower trying to scrub it off. She read how Mary Quant had her pussy dyed green and shaved into a love-heart and I held my legs up in the air while she took to me with nail scissors.

We got invited to parties where we didn't know anyone. We stole wine from the kitchen and drank it outside sitting on car bonnets with stereos thumping. Babe necked with strangers and I threw up in the bushes. We scored lifts from people who thought her clothes were weird and I was some kind of freak beneath the makeup and paint. We shared hangovers and breakfasts. We made toast and cut it into triangles and took it back to eat in bed. If I had left an extra ridge of jam dripping off my slice after buttering it I would let Babe lick the corner. I watched her tongue licking the burnt crust. Burnt because whatever I try to cook ends up burnt. But when Babe made toast it came out golden brown and white in the middle. Perfect toast, always.

And I could say, come back to my place. And with the lights off we could manage something, achieve a certain grace, because that's the difference between a big house and a small one. In a big house it is a long walk from the lounge to the bedroom – but in a small place all it takes is a nudge. All you have to do is lean across and shut your eyes. You don't have to say a word. The next morning you can cook breakfast and carry it back to bed before it gets cold. You never have to put clothes on to answer the phone – you can spend the whole day naked if you want because there are no hallways or stairs or a backyard. Two voices can fill up a whole house.

I press my face against the cold glass window to watch the car's shadow jumping and shrinking against hills and sidings. I trace my finger on the car window, on the Standards Authority branding. The Standards Authority branding tells me the window is safe, the car is safe, the road is safe and nothing can possibly go wrong. I rest my cheek against the cold smooth glass. Babe is a great driver. Normally I am nervous in cars but when she drives I feel like curling up and going straight to sleep.

The landscape flashes by.

— *SEVEN* —

'You awake?'

We are the only ones on the road. The car rumbles like its big old engine is bored, with nothing to overtake. The fuel gauge says empty.

Sure I am. She rubs my neck.

'Lazybones.'

I'm tired. I went to sleep in the sun. How far is it?

'Not far. What's this place like, anyway? Are you allowed to tell me? Or is that part of the deal?'

It's a great place.

'Well it has to be right. It's for my birthday.'

I know it will be. The rooms are huge and you can fit six people in a bed and the baths are a proper depth and the hot water is endless because it's thermal, it comes up from the ground and they heat it with gas as well. There's colour TV with cable channels and a video channel that plays soft-porn at four in the morning. The tables in the dining room are covered with starched white cloths. The foyer walls are plastered with flags – racing pennants and screenprinted native birds and visitors' business cards. They have this duckpond out the back, ringed with ferns and a garden of rocks and pebbles and it's lit up at night in blue and red and yellow, and the ducks go to sleep in the different colours, tuck their beaks under their wings.

Babe smiles. 'Sounds pretty classy.'

Hey, I know what it *is*, but they do everything for you and there's plenty of it and that's what motels are about.

'Motel? I thought you said it was a hotel.'

No, I said motel. Is there any difference? Playing with the radio, we are just out of range of the city stations. Do you still have your tattoo?

'Of course I do.'

Are you going to keep it forever?

'They fade, eventually. The ink spreads as it grows through the new skin.'

So one day it won't be there.

'It'll be softer, but it will still be there. Smudged.' She frowns. 'What's this place called?'

The Mirage.

'Is it new?'

I went there years ago, and it was old then. I don't think they've changed a thing. They can't afford to. How many people come and stay at a place out here? We count the billboards and gas stations, the old diesel pumps and single postboxes at the end of long dirt driveways. I used to wonder what it would be like growing up in a place like this, with no one around. The only people who come to stay at places like this are people from town, because they don't really know what it's like. Stuck out here without TV.

'Oh come on.'

I know. But I... feel that. Out here.

'It's quiet at night. You can see all the stars.'

I like hearing people around.

'I know what you mean.'

Do you ever get scared, driving by yourself?

'When?'

At night. Do you think bad things are going to happen if you stop?

The sun glares on the dash. 'I don't like stopping at night unless I have to. I read about enough cases as it is.' She shakes her head. 'A friend of mine at work got stopped and beaten up really badly.'

I saw a programme about this woman who was driving at night through someplace in Britain and it was the time, a few years ago, there'd been these killings, women had been killed. They'd been murdered at the scene of road accidents when they stopped to help. Well this night, she was driving and saw an accident up ahead, on the road, and a man was waving her down. He was limping. He was waving for her to stop. So she thought, gee, he's hurt, I'd better pull over, and she slowed the car down. But as she got to the side of the road he ran for the driver's door and pulled it open and grabbed her and he was covered in blood. And she just screamed and hit the accelerator but he held on, grabbed her shoulders and held until he fell away. He rolled on the road, yelling. And there was an ambulance coming so she waved it over, and the ambulance stopped and she ran over to it and called the driver, and the driver got out and stuck a scalpel into her throat. The driver was the killer. Because he was in uniform he could always get drivers to stop.

'Huh.' She smiles. 'I haven't heard that one.'

People are always intimidated by uniforms. They always do what someone in uniform tells them. That's why it's so easy to impersonate doctors and policemen. People see the uniform and they stop thinking. Once you look right people believe everything you say.

If you don't, pretending is impossible. Like, Spencer Tracy was always too short and if they didn't get that right, the whole picture was ruined. He had to wear clogs all the time. For every scene where he kissed a woman they cut big bits of wood and taped them to the bottom of his shoes, so he could reach. Otherwise he couldn't get up there. That's why in portraits, the woman is always sitting down – if she's taller than the man then the whole thing looks ridiculous.

There was that actress, the German one, who was six foot three. Her husband was another actor – he was famous and the studio got

42

her to marry him for the publicity and so she could get citizenship. But she hated him because he was only five foot something and they looked ridiculous together, when they went out to openings. She ended up stabbing him when he tried to use a dildo on her. And then she committed suicide. Their daughter saw the whole thing.

Japanese actors hardly ever commit suicide. It's to do with their training: they're taught not to respect it. In the Kabuki, everything is so dressed up it doesn't matter if you're short – it's all makeup and masks, that's the tradition. And there's hardly anything on stage, just the actors and a few props. Have you ever seen it? It's so beautiful, just a screen and masks and a single room and all these people watching in the blue light, watching and appreciating and saying nothing.

'That's what I mean about the peace and quiet,' Babe says. 'Living out here. You could just watch. Brian and I were thinking about finding a place out in the country. He doesn't mind the drive and I'm not going to be working so… I don't know. Maybe it's something we'll do.'

There is a goat run along the side of the road, a rusted shed and a long wire hung with rags.

'Which way do we go here?' Babe asks, pointing at the intersection. 'Is it a left or a right?'

It was a long time ago. I don't even remember this part. I think one way is long and the other way is a little shorter, but not by much. I think you can go either way. You might as well.

Babe stops at the Give Way for a little while, the engine idling, and then the wheel turns slowly in her hands.

— EIGHT —

At the Mirage the curtains are drawn over the ranch sliders and the sign lights are burning in the afternoon sun, bright wires beneath VACANCIES HOT TUBS SKY ELECTRIC BLANKETS. Apart from a dirty ute and white painted lines the gravel carpark is empty. We probably passed everyone on the way down and didn't even see them. It's like that when you drive for a long time, your mind wanders and you stop recognising stuff. Babe stretches her legs. The duckpond will still be out back, behind the main building, you'll see it at night when they turn the spots on. The bushes are waiting to be cut back after summer and the wooden railings are bone-dry.

I walk along to the booking office and hit the buzzer, which pisses off the manager but he wasn't looking up or anything, he was watching a football game in the office with his back to me and I feel stupid waiting ages for people to turn round. He is skinny with a funny haircut and he talks down to me like I'm a little girl. I tell him about the booking but he doesn't remember, he hasn't even written it down and he starts making a fuss about it. He goes on and on like someone's grandmother, fuck. Babe starts to come in but I promise to sort it out. She goes back and waits by the car. The manager is starting up a real argument. There is a crutch leaning on the desk, I think he's a bit funny or something. I explain again more slowly and he finally lets me have a room – when it was mine in the first place anyway, Christ. But then it is more expensive than it was going to be so I have to use Babe's cheque, which is really embarrassing and then he starts hassling her about ID and credit and stuff, it's terrible. I start to argue and he says well go somewhere else if you want, they'll require the same ID. So we sign but I think his attitude really sucks and I'm gonna complain about it later. Although I don't know who you complain to about managers.

He gives us cabin five, right at the end with a brass camel on the doorknob, and Babe watches him walk back to the office. 'What's wrong with his leg?' she says holding back the curtains. 'He looks really weird.'

I reckon it's artificial. He has big shoulder muscles – see? – like he's used to pushing himself around in a wheelchair all day. Babe nods.

Everything is smaller than it was last time, they've put in false ceilings or something. But the decor is the same and they still have the same paintings, the camel train leaving tracks in the desert near the bathroom and the black Japanese fishing boats in the sunset above the bed. They're such cool paintings. If I painted it would be paintings like that.

'Will a whole surprise party fit in here?' Babe wonders, opening and shutting the cupboards. 'I mean if we only want to sit around and talk... These tea-bags are really old. Did we bring tea-bags?' I didn't bring anything. She rinses two dishes and starts stacking them with fruit. 'We'd better go out and get something. Is there a dairy round here?'

I don't remember.

Babe shakes her hair loose. 'We'll have to get some things. Otherwise there'll be nothing to eat. Okay? Come on.'

I'm tired.

'Come on, there's a place down the road.'

Can we drive?

'No, we're going to walk, it's five minutes away.'

It's cold.

'Borrow my jacket.'

45

She throws me her leather coat, cut bum-length like an army coat. It's beautiful. The leather is cold at first but it gets warmer.

The dairy windows are covered with chipped paint signs and something yellow is dripping down the back of the refrigerator. The woman behind the counter says hello when we come in and starts talking to Babe as if they are old friends. Babe buys two big bottles of Coke and a covered dish of dip. I think the dip looks too old. 'Well you don't have to eat it,' she says. 'Choose a chocolate bar.' We choose about five between us.

Babe makes the woman go out back for fresh cheese. I spin the wire book racks. In between faded paperbacks there are rows of old magazines unread – *True Romance Fiction*, *Flying Saucer*, *True Detective Stories*. I really like the *Hot Couples* magazine, I like the readers' forum. Babe says the letters are made up but they all seem different to me, I guess they must be written by the same person but, it's possible isn't it? I mean this one here about the chicken drumsticks, would you think that up? I think it'd be easier to do it and then write about it afterwards than to think it up sitting at a desk in an air-conditioned office.

'Come on, they make it up – you know they do. Look at all these contributing editors.' She runs her finger down the names. 'They don't actually edit anything – they're the ones who write the letters.'

There are about fifty contributing editors. Well, I guess they do write it. There are so many of them. But if all the contributing editors sit in the same office together, like what do they talk about? Do they have group discussions about what things they're going to put into the letters or do they make it up separately? And what does this guy, the supervising editor do? Does he go round the desks every morning and say well we'd like a little more cocksucking this month, or breasts are definitely last year's thing. And if he does police what everyone else is writing, who tells him what to do? Does he have research done or does he just put in the sort of sex he likes himself? Is it possible for a contributing editor to go too far? Would you get fired for being too dirty, or not dirty enough? I can imagine you getting fired for being too decent about it. And whereas most companies have really flirtatious office parties I think the *Hot Couples* office parties would be really civil and everyone would go home separately. It's hard to imagine the home life. If the kids were off school they couldn't exactly come to work with you.

And what if someone who reads the magazine *does* write a letter in about sleeping with their schoolteacher or something, what then? Do the contributing editors add little bits to it to make it more dirty or do they take the dirty bits out? Do they reject it because it isn't in their style? See what I mean? When you think about it, it's kind of *more* likely that people just write in about sleeping with their schoolteacher and a whole bunch of contributing editors do the work of checking the spelling and with-holding names and addresses by request. Doesn't it seem more likely? I think a lot of them are real.

'Shall we get bread?' Babe wonders. 'They've got wholemeal.'

She isn't even listening. The shopkeeper is straightening the chip packets. I slip the magazine down the front of my jeans and walk out into the fresh air and leave Babe to choose whatever she wants. The roadside grass grows through dead wood and tyres.

The manager is waiting on the deck in his socks, his curls tangled.

'Call for you,' he says. 'Before.'

Who was it?

'A guy… Howard.' He unfolds a tiny square of paper into two, then four, then six, and squints at his own writing.

Really?

'Says please call back.' He holds it out. 'City number.'

Thanks.

'Says it's urgent.'

The paper is damp in my palm.

'You can use the office phone. Call direct.'

I'll take care of it.

'Sure? He said you *have* to ring back.'

Thank you.

'Okay.'

The flyscreen bangs shut behind him.

Babe catches up behind me. I drop it on the gravel. What sort of bread did you end up getting, anyway?

The manager watches us all the way to our cabin. He sits on the other side of the mesh at the wide, bare desk, his crutch leaning against the wall. He's such an old perve. He winked at me before.

NINE

I flop on the bed and tug my boots off, wiggle my toes in the socks with the holes in them. We should clean up, really, but we're hardly dirty. When I find the remote there is a Marilyn Monroe movie on, the one where she's in love with the two guys in drag. The only extra channel is showing football.

I love those old movies that finish with the big swell of music and someone riding off into the sunset with THE END, a real whizz-bang finale and the audience claps and it's all over. All of Marilyn Monroe's movies are like that. I guess her life was like that too. It must have been amazing being her and then leaving behind all those secrets, all the stuff she wasn't meant to know – the stuff about the Black Dahlia Murders and Jack Ruby and being on the inside with all the Kennedy brothers and the mafia and the CIA.

'I read an excellent book on the CIA,' Babe says. She lies on her stomach with a bag of chips and we talk and eat all through the movie, like she tells me some more stuff about the Kennedy assassination that I didn't know, how Lee Harvey Oswald was short-sighted and not even a very good shot.

'In all the photos of him as a young man he's wearing glasses – but in all the later photos that the CIA released to the press they couldn't have him wearing glasses because people wouldn't believe that someone with glasses could be a crack marksman and kill a president. So they had all the photographs retouched, and they went through all his family photo albums and tore out all the photos of him wearing glasses and destroyed the negatives so there were none left. Which is a shame because with glasses on Lee Harvey Oswald looked a little bit like James Dean – he looked really fragile and vulnerable. Normally' – she makes pointy shapes with her fingers – 'he wore these cute little horn-rims.'

Babe talks some more about Lee Harvey Oswald, how you can tell that photo of him holding the rifle and the socialist newspaper was faked because the shadows on his nose go in a different direction to the shadows cast by his body. 'And that's the thing about Lyndon Johnson, too, a lot of his photos were faked to make it look like he was taller than he really was. In order to secure the Texan vote.'

On the TV Marilyn is playing the ukelele and she sounds better than the whole orchestra put together and she's going to marry the millionaire, which I think becomes the sequel. I thought it was really incredible how no one ever went digging for more after she died, no one ever sorted through the clues. My favourite photograph of Marilyn Monroe is that one of her taken at a press conference. She's sitting wearing a short dress in the middle of all these journalists and the men are all laughing and looking really excited and she's smiling for the camera and it looks like a normal photograph until you realise she's not wearing any panties. It's a very famous photo because it was originally printed in newspapers and magazines without anyone noticing. You can look at the photo for ages and not see her cunt. You have to want to see it before you can.

★

'No sign of anyone yet.'

Babe lets the curtains fall.

'What time is it?'

Not late.

The sun went down quick, dropped behind the hills leaving the hotel sign lonely and bright. Further down the road is a gas station and a block of shops and a takeaways all lit up by floods, and a line of utes and dirty cars and trailbikes. The air is cold. There is only news on TV, and on the other channel is football.

'Do you think they know where to find it?'

I'm sure they do. Relax.

She stares out through the curtains. 'It's dark.'

I used to work nights at the Easter Show: Thursday nights at the candyfloss stall. I wound sugar on dirty blonde sticks. It was as dark as it is now. The gates had started to close and the lights around the ferris wheel were switching off and the PA was telling families to go home but come back tomorrow as they crossed the grass, stepping over crushed cups and cold batter hot-dogs. My job was to shut the booth and take apart the candyfloss machine and scrape the nozzles clean of dried pink sugar. But this night I hadn't even started because I was too busy watching Wayne standing by the shooting gallery.

Wayne was waiting for the stall owners to finish bolting up the cover boards. And then one of the stallholders said something about me, made a joke out loud, and that was it, Wayne dropped everything and whacked them. He went for them both. They didn't even see it coming, he beat the shit out of them, slapping their heads against the boards and left them lying. But he still came over to give me the panda. He introduced himself and I stared at his swollen face. No one ever got into a fight because of me before. It was just so fucking amazing I couldn't believe it. He said maybe we could go to a movie or something. I said that would be good. He recited my phone number and said he wouldn't forget it and walked off. The panda felt sticky in the dark. Big John.

He picked me up most days after school. His car was a rusty heap of shit with a chrome exhaust down one side. It did not have a warrant or registration or hubcaps or tyre-tread. It did have a re-bored engine block and a hand-brake. The clutch was hair-trigger: you started it by rolling down hills or by pushing and the first revs sounded like backfires piled on top of each other. It broke every written and unwritten school rule of young female conduct just being parked opposite the gates. Five minutes before the bell rang it was surrounded by six hundred giggling classmates. It was a car that gave you hickies if you so much as looked at it. When we overtook the bus Big John throttled back for a moment to let the other girls see his decorated knuckles reaching under my skirt, squeezing. And better yet when his car stopped outside the same gates *the following morning*, my creaking passenger door yawned open, my eyes were red and my skirt wasn't pressed. Because Big John and I had sex. Nights of sex, bad sex, fucking, sucking sex, screaming kick the walls and dig-your-nails-in sex. My friends stayed behind for music lessons while we drove home and stuck our tongues in everything. When he dropped me off in the mornings I ached.

Summer that year was the hottest on record, two degrees higher per day on average. We kept the curtains drawn and the windows shut all day. We made cinnamon toast and then sat down to watch TV and there was a western on. I love westerns. And this one starred John Wayne and I looked up at Wayne and said – *Big John*. He didn't say anything. By the end of the week everyone was calling him Big John. That's when his nickname stuck – in the heat.

There is a noise from outside.

'Someone's coming,' Babe says. The car stops and the engine stops and there is talking and laughing and the doors slam as people get out. Their weight shakes the board steps leading up to the office. There are a couple of them and they sound drunk. They belt on the office door. They're gonna wake the guy up. Fuck, he deserves to be woken up.

'Listen…' And she stops to count the vehicles following – three in all crunching loose metal and slamming their doors. The lights are coming on in the reception office by this time and the funny man with the curly hair is telling everyone to be quiet over the noise.

Babe drags on the cigarette. Her eyes are shining in the weak light.

'It's them.' She starts to smile.

They are all drunk and talking and roaming along the balcony walkway and arguing with the manager about the price of the rooms and laughing about how late they are and blaming the weather and the drive down. Music swells from the car tape decks when they open the doors. Babe slides off the bed and straightens her shirt.

'Should we go to the door? Or should we wait? Am I allowed to know? I don't know what to do. Am I supposed to be asleep?'

They are all crowding into the office now, giggling. She walks to the window and peeks out the curtain, her shoulders hunched. 'It's so dark. I can hardly see them.' She pushes the curtains aside more. 'How many did you invite? There's about twenty people.' She presses her nose against the glass. 'Trina there's...' She stays with her face against the glass. 'There's...' She shades her reflection with her hand. 'The cars are all new. Did they rent cars? They...'

She lifts her hand higher. She stares out the window at the booking office and watches the people packed into it, the people spilling out, the people she doesn't know. Just strangers.

Some of them are Japanese I think. Babe looks at them one by one to be sure, shading her reflection with her hand. Someone taps on the glass and she lets the curtains fall. She finds herself an orange in the fruitbowl and runs over its skin with her fingertip. The tip of her cigarette glows in the dim room.

'It wasn't them. Did you think it was?'

I thought it might have been.

'You looked surprised.'

53

Did I?

She slowly peels the orange over the bench. She holds the cigarette in her mouth. It looks bloody awful, your cigarette hanging out like that. It looks sloppy.

'Is there something you're not telling me?' she asks, softly.

What do you mean?

'It's just that you had that look on your face that you get sometimes.'

What look?

She breaks the orange open with her thumbs. 'They are coming, aren't they? Everyone is meeting us here for my party, right?'

We did talk about it.

'Did you?'

We said how it would be nice to get away for the weekend. We thought about booking a whole lot of places, and I suggested here, and I thought it would be good. Because I really think you need to take a break from things. You're working all the time and we hardly see you, none of us do. And soon you won't feel like travelling, and then you'll have everything else to deal with...

I thought it would be good. I had it all planned. The others *were* interested. I did *tell* them. They do *know*. I mean, we're going to have a good time. We always find stuff to do. We always have. I think we'll have a great time. Regardless.

The orange on the plate has gone. Babe watches me. Her hands are folded in her lap.

I thought it would be good.

She switches off the lights and goes into the bathroom. I can hear the shower running. I could get up and turn on the lights but I don't feel like it, not just yet. I sit in the dark wondering if I should open the window so all the cigarette smoke has somewhere to go.

TEN

When I was a kid, I used to dream. Once I had the flu and my fever was so high I could only half-sleep in bed. I dozed propped up with pillows. When I opened my eyes the room was dark and there was a man waiting for me at the end of the bed dressed in a monk's cloak with a hood over his head. I didn't know who he was, his face was hidden by the darkness and the brown cloth. I was so afraid I wanted to scream but my throat was swollen and I could barely breathe let alone call out. All I could do was sit up holding the sheets to my neck and watching him. Finally he held out a little stainless steel measuring cup and gestured for me to take it. He was there to give it to me. I shook my head because I thought it contained poison. He didn't say anything, just gently held the phial closer. I tried sitting and waiting but I was too nervous and finally I gave in and drank it. All it turned out to be was medicine, the sweet stuff with alcohol in it that I liked. After I finished the man nodded and sat with his hands resting in his lap, and I fell asleep. When I woke up for real he was gone and my fever was worse than before, it was raging.

When I wake up Babe is sitting at the bottom of the bed, her chin in her hands. The refrigerator hums. I am warm in the bed and my mouth is dry. The clock says one in the morning.

'You were so sound asleep,' Babe says. 'Your face was perfectly still.'

Was I?

She nods. 'Do you want some tea?' She doesn't look angry. 'I made some.'

So I sit up, white with one sugar thanks. She nods at the plastic cup. 'I was worried there weren't going to be enough.'

Yes.

'I really thought it was the manager. I thought he'd just forgotten...'

Is there any chocolate left?

'A bit.' She pushes the silver paper in her lap, picking up the scraps with her licked fingertip.

The manager has freckles, liver spots. The Boston strangler had freckles – he covered them with women's makeup when he went out, he was so embarrassed. Pancake. He killed because he hated his skin – he hated women's skin, the feel of it. He strangled wearing leather gloves. And he only killed women who were fair-skinned. Did you know that?

Babe relaxes, she lets her shoulders fall forward.

'Why did you say everyone was coming?'

I thought they would.

'You didn't, really.'

I did. We had talked about it. I thought there was going to be a party. And then all the way down here I was thinking to myself, thinking you know, those guys probably aren't gonna come. They must be busy or something, they forgot. It's typical, right? They never turn up.

'They came to your party last year.'

That was a great party. We hired a place and had a sound system and a proper bar and I got so drunk. I had to sit outside throwing up for half of it. Babe sat with me.

'You were really sick.'

I was okay.

'Shall we go back tomorrow?'

No. I don't want to go back to town. Not just yet.

I tuck my feet under her soft curves thickened by sheets. Her hair is so long it comes down past her waist.

'You should grow yours.' She stares slow. 'You've got beautiful hair.'

She used to put waves in it with curlers and a hairdryer. She would tease it up, spray it. And it went stiffer when it had a colour through it.

'It used to take hours. God.'

I loved that. I loved when she did my hair. She used to do it with highlights and shaved up the sides, mohican.

'I thought you hated it.'

No. I loved when you made me blonde.

'It looked strange.'

No, it was great.

'Was it?' Babe smiles. When you leant over the sink with the hot water running forward, your eyes red and itching.

Do my hair, Babe.

'It's a bit late.'

It's barely one o'clock. We'd still be getting ready to go out at one, still be putting on the finishing touches. She complains she hasn't brought anything with her, but I have. I slide it out from under the bed.

'Is that my makeup case?' She snaps the locks open. 'God. It's my old case. You kept it.'

I still use the eye shadows.

'You do not, you never wear makeup. Trina. Wow.'

She goes through the colours and brushes and pencil stubs. I kept it. It's the sort of thing you never throw out because it might come in useful. You never know when you're gonna get dressed up. I need to pee, excuse me a sec. The cold porcelain seat. Maybe I should grow my hair. When I hold it up it looks good in the mirror… like that. But it gets stupid and fluffy. There's sleep in my eyes after only maybe an hour. Cold water running.

Babe is still sitting on the bed when I go back, the pots and trays spread out on the sheets. Aren't they great? All the colours. This one's nice, this one's great. But it's not as dark. And this one. Do my makeup, Babe. Please? We could go out.

'Where to, the gas station?'

Do my makeup.

'Your face is dirty.'

I washed it. I'll wash it again.

'I'm tired.'

Do my makeup.

'Trina.'

Please.

'Well… You'll have to take it off again.'

I don't mind.

She clicks on the bedside lamp. I want to lie down, which isn't the proper way but I'm tired, so she makes me lie with the light right between my eyes. She squeezes a tiny sponge in her fist.

'How do you want this? Heavy? It's just gonna make a mess… There are false eyelashes here, you know. Okay. This stuff is so black. Well, it's practically black. It's dried… there's some stuff down the end… There's some other stuff – this stuff – that's fresh. Look, it's still fresh. Smell? Okay. Look up… at the top of the bed… Good and the other… Okay. Now look down.'

Her breath smells of chocolate. Her hand is heavy with the small wet brushes, pressing my eyeballs through their lids. She purses her lips to blow dust off jars. I lie in the pillow feeling my face wet and tighten into a new shape, heavy and dark with a small sharp jaw, and my eyes tickle with the new lashes and my nose tingles, my whole face feels like jewellery, like I shouldn't move it too fast and Babe rattles in the box, goes through containers, gets tissues from the bathroom. Can I open my eyes yet?

'The mascara's wet.'

When can I look?

'Not till I've finished.'

When will you be finished?

'Ages and ages.' She steadies her fingers on my cheek so she can draw a straight line. 'Now be still.'

★

'...I had this workman once. Just a young guy. He was putting drains in along the fence, in the property next door. We watched them from the window...'

You and who else?

'Just a friend. We watched them and picked him because he was the youngest. He was still a virgin. He said he wasn't but he was so nervous he had to be.'

Did you sleep together?

'I sucked him off. On the kitchen table. He squealed. Like a little pig. He tried to ring later but we hung up. It was just for fun.' Babe turns my face in the light, her pencil following the eyelid curve. 'Just something you do, you know?'

How many men have you slept with?

'Lost count.'

Really?

'No.' She smiles. 'I remember.'

How many?

'Enough.'

I've hardly slept with any.

'Crap.' She slaps my ear. 'You are in a mood. Other side...'

I can see the lightbulbs with my eyes shut, shining through the red skin. There haven't been so many, really.

Being stroked wakes up the skin of my face. Makeup reminds you. Each layer highlights what's missing, what's been. Someone sees you made up and thinks, she's pretty, but you know what went into it and it doesn't feel pretty at all. That's why people become different after makeup – their face changing reminds them of who they are. Your face is retraced along the lines of what you've been through and the lines lead back to who you are now.

'I never thought of it like that.'

I bet you did.

'I don't think that much about it.' The sponge pads my face as soft as warm mud. Babe is busy concentrating, I think this is the first time I have seen her so content. She is always happy when she is doing something for people, like making them breakfast or combing their hair or doing their face. She's such a mother. She's going to be a great mother. She's going to run after her kid all the time and be one of those mothers who never puts their kids down. I can see it. She combs my hair back behind my ears and touches up my nose again. She shows me how to hold my mouth so she can trace the upper lip. The lipstick smells of old wax. She's going to do this for her daughter someday, she'll be doing her makeup all the time. She blows dust off the curling tongs and plugs them into the socket.

★

'There.' Babe sits back. 'You look amazing.'

Do I?

'You really do.'

Can I get up?

'Sure. You got a cigarette?'

Is it dry? I thought you said you were going to give up.

'I earned it, I'm tired.' She goes through my packet and lights one and pulls on it and squints at her work. 'Your eyes are still a bit sticky, don't open them too much. Here.' She finds a pocket mirror. 'Look.'

Wow.

'You like it?'

It's how I used to do it.

'Careful, don't touch.'

It's so thick. I look fifty years old and a millionaire.

'Now you can take it off and go to bed,' she laughs.

I'm never going to take it off.

Babe sits holding her eyebrow pencil. In the mirror I look older and sharper. I look drawn with a hand steadier than mine, eyebrows black, eyelines black, eyes black, lips black, hair black. Babe slides off the bed and straightens her shirt and goes to wash her hands. Face white, hands white, teeth white, nails white. Babe watches me from the bathroom mirror and smiles.

— ELEVEN —

A long time ago I remember looking in the mirror and wondering how it reflected. The only thing on the back was dark red paint which I didn't believe could reflect anything. I liked how you could tilt the mirror and knock your reflection off its feet.

Once Babe made me up like this and we went dancing. It was late and a Saturday and everything was full, and we ended up in some dive at the top of town sharing a table with these Russian sailors. They were into dancing and bought us drinks constantly so after a few hours we were pretty spinny and in a good mood. Babe was off somewhere. I wasn't used to that, I was used to being with her. One of them said I've got something if you want, come downstairs, and I went with him into the street out back and we had half each. For a long time nothing happened, and then it didn't seem to matter how long time took, how long we waited.

It was the Russian guy's last night here and he started telling me how he didn't want to go back home. He came from a town in the north of Russia where they make all the rods for nuclear reactors. They mine the uranium up in the mountains and bring it down to this particular place and make it into rods which are then shipped out in big cement containers to all the power plants in Russia. This guy was in charge of checking the concrete containers. He said in the seventies, when Russia had lots of money, the containers were made very carefully, but now the government was trying to get by with less and made the containers using as little cement as possible. He said the containers were now no thicker than his finger and often they were cracked or open at one side because the panels of cement hadn't been poured correctly. He said the whole town was radioactive now, everyone was sick with it. He said he went back to visit his girlfriend and she looked 20 years older than him. She looked like a stranger.

I remember he had bad teeth but he was proud of his fillings. He pulled his lip out with his fingers to show me all the metal in his teeth. Dental work is very expensive in Russia but everyone from his town had good dental work – they made the fillings out of the old uranium. He said his whole mouth was radioactive, just a little bit. He said, kiss me and see what happens. Afterwards I went inside the ladies room and looked at myself in the mirror and it was like a different person staring back.

When the Christians kept people prisoner in the Crusades they would put masks on them in jail so that no one could tell who the prisoners were. That way you couldn't complain to the authorities if there was someone in jail who you knew had been improperly arrested, and you couldn't know who was being held where if you wanted to storm the prison and release them. When the prisoners were released and their masks taken off they would have forgotten what they looked like. And when the prisoners' families came to collect them, they wouldn't recognise each other. Usually the prisoners' wives would have taken up with someone else, which makes you wonder how much they needed to be married in the first place.

They also invented chastity belts for the Crusades. I don't think they really worked. I spent a long time trying to work it out and I can't see really how you can manage to shit and piss when you're wearing steel pants, let alone have your period. Even if they only have a hoop and a belt it's still pretty inconvenient, and I think anyone with a lock on their stomach every night and day for three years would start to figure a way of picking it. There was one queen who worried about her husband so much she lost weight and the thing just fell off. She stepped out of it and had a good time for three years. It wasn't that she had a lot of lovers but she had a lot of friends and she could do all the things she wasn't supposed to do by herself, like reading and riding and hanging round taverns and stuff. Then when her husband wrote to say he was returning she tried to get her chastity belt back on and found she'd become too fat to slip into it again, on account of all the mead and cakes and ale. And so she really started to worry then, and of course went off her food and lost weight and just managed to get the thing back on before the king got back. But even if that hadn't happened I think she should have been able to figure her way out of it if she really wanted to.

— TWELVE —

Babe is cupping herself in her fingers, measuring her reflection. Soon she will ripen to a pear curve. She turns on her heel to imagine the shape she will be – she lifts her chin a little. The curve of her neck and her gentle shoulders, the tiny black stem of a gap between her thighs. The tattoo shimmers on her tailbone. She smiles as I bump past and sit knock-kneed to pee. She toys with the tiny snick of gold in her nipple, tipping it on a finger's end.

It's not real gold, is it?

'Eighteen carat.'

Have you taken it out before?

'Not for awhile. It's grown in and got infected.'

Youch.

'Only slightly. It was sore when it first got done and it hurt for months after that, every time I touched it. I thought I'd really done it, ruined something. Your body remembers.' I look worried and she rolls her eyes. 'If you can't handle it...'

It's better if I wash my hands first.

'You're not taking out my appendix or anything.'

I don't want to leave a scar.

'It's only a little hole.'

I read about a woman who let old mascara cake up so much that a chip of it scarred her retina. They fix eyes with lasers now, heat-stitch them. Under local anaesthetic. But that must give you a headache. I got a headache even after the x-ray.

'Medicine.' She sniffs. 'It's so bad for you.'

During the French revolution old ladies used to take boys into theatre boxes and jerk them off and rub the come into their faces because come makes the skin tight, with all the minerals. It made them look young for the evening. But you can't do that now. I mean, you could if you'd both had blood tests and were married to someone. But then you wouldn't need to take someone to the theatre to do it, if you were married. They don't even have theatre boxes now. You'd have to do it at the pictures.

She laughs. She looks at us side by side in the mirror, our toes touching. 'Your skin's so smooth.' She dabs at my eyelids. 'You look beautiful.'

I used to wear makeup like this all the time.

'I know.'

I used to wear it in summer, thick foundation and I remember sweating through it, it was like wallpaper paste. This summer felt as if it was raining even when there were no clouds. The rain would come and you'd think, thank God, the weather's broken, and then it would go away again – and the humidity would be worse than ever. I came out in lumps. When I went to the doctor he said it was tomatoes but it wasn't tomatoes at all. I was allergic to the whole weather, to the air.

'Lead in the air and the power lines and processed food. It's poisonous. You shouldn't live in the city. I don't know how you do it. And now people breaking in.'

I know.

'Well…?' She touches my shoulder.

Okay.

She tears off some tissues like it's going to bleed buckets.

'It's not. Don't be such a child.' She sits on the formica sink-top, leaning back under the single light. I wash my hands anyway and hold her nipple. The ring moves but only slightly, there is a piece of flesh around it, half-coloured like the moon on a fingernail. I lick my thumb to soften the skin, thinking I could maybe push it back with something.

The rose-bruise, grey veins feathered outwards, a pool's ripple.

In the makeup box is a nail file with a flat edge for pushing back cuticles. I think it will do. See?

'That looks fine.'

I'll try.

'Ow...'

Is that hurting?

'It's okay. Ow.'

It's gonna hurt.

'Just do it quickly before it hurts.'

I press with the metal edge, and the nipple flesh pops back along the ring and a dot of blood appears and swells before a break appears in the metal and I can twist the ring apart into a C-shape and it comes away. Babe lets her breath out and presses the tissue against her nipple. I drop the ring on the side of the sink. It nearly falls but I catch it. It nearly falls down the drain and is lost forever.

Her eyes are watering like it really smarts. I dab her with warm water until there is nothing there. She's laughing because it hurt. And then I kiss it, the coarse dark skin under my lips shuddering in the fluorescent light. And I wait.

Babe does nothing, leaning back against herself in the mirror, closing her eyes to my mouth on her nipple, the gentle sucking and my hands in the small of her back holding her close.

Babe's mouth against the glass, thinking to herself, long slow licks.

'Catrina...'

Her palms lift me away and smooth my temples and then she picks up the hairbrush and combs my hair. She licks my eyebrows flat and gives me her t-shirt and walks me back to bed with her arm over my shoulder. She falls asleep holding my hand and saying nothing.

★

The bathroom light is burning in the mirror.

Babe.

My makeup is sticking to the pillow.

Babe?

I shin the bedside table and the dead heater hisses. The curtains feel damp from the rain, cool to touch. As I stand they bump my legs in the breeze, moved by the empty night air.

The sun is still a long way away, underneath the hills. My face is dark in the window glass, the makeup thick as cream. The Japanese are partying next door, singing karaoke, drinking and talking, jet lag I guess. Their room lights shine through the rain.

Adults never go to sleep when they should. When kids get tired they drop down anywhere and shut their eyes – they're either running or unconscious. The older you get the more you find yourself stuck in between. You stay awake because there's something to do or someone to talk to, and when you do get to bed you dream or don't sleep because you're worried, and in the morning you're still tired but have to get up anyway. You end up halfway between day and night and not enjoying either.

The older I got, the less I slept. I would get up after bedtime to watch television through the crack in the lounge door. Everyone knew I was doing it but they let me stay there. They figured I'd fall asleep sooner or later but I didn't, I stayed and watched programmes for hours through a half-inch gap. When I got to watch the whole screen it was never as good. The gap made everyone look so tall on the black and white, tall and skinny and beautiful.

— *THIRTEEN* —

First thing in the morning, Babe wakes up and runs to the bathroom to vomit.

Do you want anything?

I can get you anything.

She hunches over the toilet, retching, her cheeks red. Sick on her hair hangs in strands.

She asks me not to stroke her back, so I stop.

We did talk about the surprise party. We did. It was gonna be something like this. Some place. Okay? It was going to be like this.

It felt right.

Oh God.

We can go home soon if you want. We can go home now after breakfast.

You're so pale.

If you want a doctor the manager can call one, I'm sure. I can't believe you're like this every morning. Well, I can't. Not without a party the night before, right?

She goes back to bed and pulls the sheets up around her neck. I wring out a hot flannel and wipe her face.

That's cool, isn't it? That feels good. Pressed on your face. I love a hot flannel. My grandmother used to wipe my face with a hot flannel. When she was alone she used to cry. I didn't know what to do about it. For a long time I thought it was something I'd done. It never occurred that she would get upset over someone other than me. She was so professional when she spoke with other people. Hearing her chat with the grocer was like listening to a stranger, she was so collected. I forget his name. He moved away after a time but she never got sentimental over it. Other people never rattled her.

It was a long time ago.

Are you feeling better now?

You should sleep.

I'm sorry Babe.

I'll clean everything.

★

The rain is spitting. I walk slowly in the fresh air. The dining room windows are steamed up. The people inside – the same ones that came in last night – are still shouting and laughing. The manager waves to me from the office.

'Another call,' he says. 'After midnight.'

Did it get you out of bed? I'm sorry.

'Told them to ring back.' He hands me the note. 'We don't put calls through that late. Who's up at that hour, eh?'

Yeah. Well. Thanks.

'You can come and use the office phone if you want.'

Maybe after breakfast.

'The number's there.'

I put the note in my pocket. Thanks.

'No problem. If they ring back…'

Actually, my friend's a bit sick this morning, so maybe you should hold our calls.

'Not well, is she?'

Just a cold. But if you just take a message, that would be great. He says he is happy to do that. The fly screen squeaks shut again. He watches me from behind the door. I pull up my collar and run across the gravel.

'Theo.' He holds out his hand.

Hi.

'Pleased to meet you, Catrina.'

He wears a baseball cap and a hunting jacket. He has food caught in his gold front tooth. He goes through his jacket pockets. 'You want some chocolate?' he says. 'I got some chocolate here somewhere.'

Not before breakfast.

'So you girls been staying here long?'

We came in yesterday.

'Pretty formal for breakfast.'

My reflection sits on his shoulder, the smudged girl, false eyelashes and her hair teased, checkered tablecloths, people queuing on the food counter. He wonders:

'You from round here?'

My friend lives just over the hill.

'Is that so.'

Her family live there. She's from a farm, originally.

'And are you a farming girl?'

No. I'm from the city.

'But you're staying here.'

Her family's having this big family reunion at the farmhouse and they kind of ran out of beds.

'Don't like her parents, huh?'

It's not that.

'Don't like your choice in friends?'

What friends?

'You meeting someone here, right?' He runs his finger around

71

his eye, pointing at my makeup. That makes me smile. You got it wrong.

'Have I?'

Yep.

'In that case…' he tips his baseball cap, '…I do beg your pardon.'

Is that your home team? On your cap. Rams. What do they play?

'Football. You been to Los Angeles?'

Nup.

'Rams play for Los Angeles.'

His breath smells of beer. He waves his big red fingers at the Japanese guys. 'They all got them. But they're not from Los Angeles.'

But you're from Los Angeles.

'Nope.'

I thought you were.

'Not from Los Angeles.' He sucks in his top lip and leans over. 'So you're not waiting for anyone?'

No.

'Well that's good.'

Why's it good? He only smiles and jiggles his drink.

'You sure you don't want one?'

It's not even lunchtime.

'Hair of the dog.'

That bit you.

'What's that?'

Hair of the dog. That bit you. It's the saying.

'That's it. That's what I said.' He shakes the can. 'You got it.'

Did your breakfast take this long?

'Haven't had any. We've been at it all night. Sorry if we kept you up.'

You were pretty quiet.

'Quiet.' He looks pleased. 'Hard to believe.'

I heard singing.

'Karaoke.'

Did you sing?

'We all sang.'

You got in late enough.

'Guy at the desk wasn't too pleased.'

He's weird.

'D'you ski?'

Sorry...?

'Do you ski? You know.' He mimes holding poles. 'Snow.'

Oh. No.

'Great powder this season.'

Is that good?

'Oh yes. That's the best.'

Is that your friend?

'Which one?'

The one throwing up.

'Oh. A-ha ha. Pete.'

Everyone is shouting and pointing.

'Pete! PETE. A-ha ha. You're messing up the place. PETE.'

God.

'Pete. Pete?' Theo shrugs. 'He'll be okay in a second.'

He should be outside.

'Is he putting you off your breakfast?'

I don't even have my breakfast. I'm still waiting.

'Well he'll probably still be going when it arrives. A-ha ha a-ha.'
Wipes his nose with the back of his hand, Jesus. 'That's just a little
joke. I was making a little joke there. A-ha.'

Yeah...

'You're a quiet one.'

What's that mean?

'Means you're quiet.'

Shouldn't you look after your friend...

'He's okay. So, you like my cap?'

It's okay.

'Well here. You have it.' He puts it on my head. 'S' big for ya. Lookit. You got just a little head.' He snaps off a piece of chocolate. 'Sure you don't want some?'

★

Wayne was standing in the kitchen drinking from a baby bottle of scotch. There were two chocolate bars lying on the sideboard in their wrappers. He offered me some but I said no. He looked at me funny when I said it. I wanted to jump off and run into my room, then. But I didn't. I made myself sit there and tell him I wanted to move out. I tried to explain how I wanted to live by myself so we could go out with each other again – we could call each other up and meet in town for coffee and go to the movies and decide afterwards whose place to stay at. The cold bench was stinging my legs. We could leave clothes at each other's house by accident. It would be like a normal relationship, it'd be fun. Don't you think?

He spat at that, he said it was a stupid fucking idea. He yelled in my face. You're all the fucking same, he said. Fucking Lorraine and fucking Alison and fucking Sharona. And I said well it's your fault for going out with girls who were all song titles. He got really pissed off then, he started banging things. You're all the same, you all lie through your teeth, you're a liar like the rest of them. You're worse than them. You're *worse*. He stalked me around the house, yelling

74

and punching walls. He smashed a whole lot of stuff, and that made it easier. I sat in the bedroom waiting for him to finish, listening to things coming off the shelves and crashing on the floor.

I thought about him with other people and that made me angry too. I stayed on that night. I slept by myself with the door locked. But I didn't stay angry. I thought saying goodbye to people you hate would be easy, but it's not. Saying goodbye to them is hard because you know you're never going to see people you hate again.

— *FOURTEEN* —

Babe lets her speech slur, lets it roll out slowly, and looks at the Rams cap with sleepy eyes. Over at breakfast. This funny guy gave it to me. He's staying with his friends. Her cheek rests against the pillow, pink on the soft white. Are you feeling better?

'I'd love some melon.'

The fruit looks green but is ripe on the inside. The pips slide from the flesh to leave a small wet crease. She chews slowly. Are you always so sick?

'Sometimes.'

I didn't think it was true. I thought it was only like that on TV.

'Yeah. Sometimes…' She laughs. 'Don't look so worried.'

I think you should eat. I scoop her up some more on the spoon. She holds it in her mouth, letting the juice run. 'It's so sweet,' she says. I can get you something proper. 'No, no.' She wipes her lips. 'This is the right thing.'

★

In the afternoon I get the pool key. She doesn't want to get out of bed but I make her come for a swim in the rain. It'll warm you up. Even just putting your feet in is enough. See? I want to splash in the water. She sits on the edge, shivering in a towel.

The cold has trapped the air in the valley like a fog. You can smell the log fires and car exhaust. The hills are almost invisible. The motel sign is bright against the road, flashing VACANCIES.

'What else did you and your friend talk about?'

We were just waiting for breakfast. It took ages. I had sausages and bacon and eggs and toast and coffee – everything.

'Your appetite's back.'

After the long drive. The air makes you hungry, maybe. She nods. Are you going to get in? You'll freeze. How's your tit?

'Swollen.' She cups it in one hand. 'Not because of you, though. You did a good job. You were gentle with it.' Maybe I should go into the tattoo business. 'Yeah.' She drops the towel and steps into the water. 'Christ, it's hot.'

Only because you're cold. She eases onto the wooden seat. When she is under she takes my foot and starts rubbing it. I still get sprains – the bones click in and out. I can never be bothered getting it seen to. It's such a fuss. I hate doctors.

It's been quite a week, with your birthday and everything. All the fuss. Everywhere I go there's a fuss. I was thinking about next year – I thought I might go back and finish my course. Over the last few years… I missed the reading. And a degree might get me a better job. Do you think? I mean, I'm living so close to town, now. I could probably even manage the work by myself… It feels really good when you rub just… there. By the heel.

If I owned this place I would be in the pool all the time. Bugger the guests. I can't believe that guy doesn't use the place. I don't think anyone does. Maybe it's got something to do with his leg. Maybe he fell in and burned himself. You know, when they first tapped into the spring. It's thermal, isn't it? That would cook your flesh right off.

Last time we came down here I bought one of those little jars of sand. You know the ones? The little test-tubes filled with layers of different coloured sands. Finally I opened it up and stirred them together.

The makeup sweats out of my pores. Do I look young again? I liked it messed up, I enjoyed looking like that. Babe wonders about that. She rubs my other foot. That feels so very good. 'Does it?' she says. She leans back against the rim, watching me splash around, her skin shining beneath the water.

— FIFTEEN —

Theo's crowd are still going, that makes it over 24 hours. The light from their cabin shines through the curtains and the music thumps through the walls. I stare at the ceiling and consider going over. I have been asleep since dinner. The sheets are damp and my neck itches. Maybe I'm getting a cold. I feel like swimming again. I could lie in the pool all night.

Hot Couples is spread on the floor, the glossy pages wobbling in the party lights. There are men being jerked off and women arching their heads back and cocksucking and women being fucked. I read about the nymphomaniac who likes three men at a time, the man who likes fists up his arse, about warm wet cunts. I read about all the things that fit in vaginas: takeaway chicken legs and champagne bottle necks and gloved fingers and boot heels. There are men who suck themselves off with vacuum cleaners. Boys are always being initiated by cleaning women and maids and maths tutors and au pairs and neighbours. Semen tastes sweet and warm and rich and bitter. All the cocks are enormous and the women stay wet forever. There is even a woman with tattoos – the tattooed lady.

As she sleeps, Babe's tattoo stares up at the wall, perched on her tailbone. When it was first finished I had to change the dressing for her – it bled until it scabbed and then later the scab fell off.

I once went out with a guy who was covered in tattoos. When he undressed he was black with them. But he never got any done on his hands or his neck. He said that's the only place you can't get tattooed. If you have them on your face you get into fights all the time – just by someone looking at you. He got blood poisoning in the end and was put into hospital. And he was deficient in Vitamin

D because the skin hidden under all the ink and scars didn't get any sun.

There was this murder case where the killers cut up a man and fed his body to the sharks, and later a shark was caught by fishermen and opened up and they found the victim's arm inside. They identified the arm by the tattoo on the bicep, and put the murderers in jail. I thought being in the stomach of a shark would eat away at your skin but evidently shark stomachs don't have a very high acidity. I guess they have a pretty low stress lifestyle when you think about it, floating in the water and eating whatever comes along. That is the way to be: big and hungry, and you just take whatever you want when you see it. You don't think twice about anything. And whatever you take, whoever it is, they wouldn't even see it coming.

The people in *Hot Couples* are still sucking and fucking, still stretched over poles and bars and steaming rods, hiked up and glistening and stroked red and moaning. They mutter and gasp and beg and throb. They fall to their knees and reach new heights of passion. They split their ripe peaches and buns and strawberry blonde bushes. I turn the pages one after the other in the dark, in my fingertips – one kiss after another, one tongue and one crack and one furrow.

★

'...Trina.'

She is breathing hard with her face down in the sheets. The panic in what she says has yet to harden. My hands are warm and her back is warm and her thighs spread like her swollen nipple. She tastes of clean salt.

'Trina stop it.'

Her hands are gradually getting a grip and her back straightens.

80

The strong parts are waking up, the difficult things, the reasons, the practical considerations, the legal aspects, the homework pinned to the wall in the sun.

'Trina stop.'

Do you remember in the sun, the grass? Wet after swimming practice and the bathroom mirror? You never have that feeling again.

She takes my wrists and she's big, she just twists right out from underneath.

I'm not going to cry. All I can do is lean forward to kiss her again. I'm not going to cry.

She fetches me one, hits me right in the face with her open hand and yells.

I catch the bedside lamp when I fall. It goes through the window and people come running.

The door jumps off its hinges and then they are on me.

★

The music is even louder inside. The cigarette smoke makes me cough. Theo and all them are still drunk but he still manages to get me down on the bed and carefully clean my head – the stitches have opened up and they hurt for the first time. All that fuss in the hospital and now, when I could really do with a hit of gas or pills or something, I'm stuck in a hotel room full of old songs and cigarettes and Rams caps. Theo hovers with a cotton wad. I think he is seeing double and trying to decide which one is me.

Later on I get up and sing, and everyone claps along. I sing:

Tall and tan and la la la lovely,

The girl from dum te dum goes something

And when she la te dum – everybody goes – Aah.

Theo laughs.

'You got a great voice.'

Have I?

'You should sing more.'

I don't know what to say. Should I?

'Of course you should.'

Then sing it with me.

He gets up and holds the microphone.

'Ready... Go!'

Tan and tall and la la la lovely,

The girl from something or other goes walking.

Theo puts his arm around me and everyone claps.

Tan and tall and la la la lovely.

Everyone wants to know what happened to my head. It was a dog. There is this big black labrador that lives next door to me. It's lovely. No no, I *like* dogs. I like him. Bruno, his name is. Listen: this is how. I always play ball with this dog, we play fetch. He's lovely. I have this big children's ball and I throw it and Bruno brings it back every time. Well a few days ago, right, we were playing in the back yard. I was sitting in the sun with my hat over my face and I threw the ball and it went into the bushes. And Bruno didn't come back for ages. He was sniffing around in the bushes going crazy. So I went and helped him look. I was rooting round in the bushes – I still had my hat on, see – and I came up suddenly and he thought my head was the ball and he bit it. He was so sorry about it. He licked me for ages. He knew he'd hurt me and he didn't know what to do.

★

Even after you have finished loving someone it is still nice to see them. When Wayne first came round he sat next to me on the couch for a long time and held my hand. It was uncomfortable sharing. My furniture is the wrong shape. When he kissed me it was short. Like a baby kiss. He didn't know what to do. I didn't know what I wanted either. We watched the gas burn in blue rows. He talked about staying but I said no, it's Babe's birthday and we're gonna meet for a drink. He looked down. Birthdays are important and you can't forget them. We're going up, me and the guys, all our varsity friends. You can come along if you want to. He knew he could. He said sorry when he left and I said, sorry for what? It could have been worse – if we'd argued, had a fight or something. And then he walked out. That was three nights ago. It seems longer.

— *SIXTEEN* —

The bedroom glows in the red hum of the fan heater. Everyone else is playing cards in the next room, shouting and jeering. Theo talks about funny things. He lies with his hands clasped behind his head and his cap over his eyes.

'You sure you're feeling okay?' he asks.

Yeah.

'You sang great.'

I used to sing in the choir.

'Aah. That's nice.'

We had a choir at school and I sang in the front row. I was one of the best. And then I strained myself and got sick. This ball of fluid swelled up in my throat, it was a cyst...

'A goitre?' He frowns.

That's what it was. It swelled up and almost stopped my breathing and I had to go into hospital. That was the week before my final exams. So I got aggregate scores and they weren't enough for my degree. I only got average scores. I needed higher.

'What really happened to your head? You've got a bad bang there.'

It's embarrassing.

'You don't have to tell me.'

I know. I was shopping. I was going out, carrying my groceries down the escalator. And I slipped. In the middle of the store, in front of everyone. I went face first into the doors.

'Jesus.'

They didn't break, but... they're strong glass. I just bruised it. I woke up lying in all my food. They wanted to call an ambulance – honest, I was going to die of embarrassment.

'That's pretty ugly,' he grins. 'Sorry. Not laughing at you.'

You should – it's funny. I laughed afterwards. Eventually.

'You've had quite a time. And your friend drinking like that…'

Babe doesn't drink that much.

'She drank enough to get up and push you pretty hard.'

She's kind of upset. In fact she's very upset. Some people were meant to come up this weekend and they didn't. It's her birthday. We had this party all arranged and they didn't come.

'What, and she's up here waiting?'

That's right. They're friends too.

'That's pretty shabby.'

Yeah.

He pushes his cap back and stares at the ceiling and then he looks over at me. He has a hard stare. Not angry, though. He stares as if he's looking for something small. 'Well, she shouldn't be by herself, your friend.'

I think she wants to be alone. Like Greta Garbo.

'She should get over here and unwind.'

She's fine, really.

'Are you scared?'

Of course I'm not scared. But…

'It's hard making up, I know that. But we should do it. You should try, at least.' He raises his eyebrows. 'A little humility. It's important. The world's a very selfish place.'

Come on.

'It is. I see it. I meet a lot of people. When I was going round Europe I had to look after myself all the time. Once I was on a bus, sitting with these young guys, locals. It was a hot day and they were sharing a can of soft drink and they offered me some. Later I fell asleep, and when I woke up my pack was gone. The whole thing. Passport, money, everything. The police said the boys had slipped me an anaesthetic in the can. It's an old trick. And I fell for it. I was totally ripped off. And that's what it's like. Everyone's out to get you. You should look after the people that aren't.'

I just don't think we should wake her up again.

'Well. Okay.' He rests back on the pillow. 'She's your friend.'

Yes.

'You known each other long?'

Years and years. Where are those guys from?

'Oh, we met up. Group booking, we got a discount. I never met them before.'

Not even Pete?

'Nah. I make friends fast. You have to – travelling.'

I guess we're friends, now.

'Guess so.'

I feel like more wine. I know I shouldn't but I feel like it. It's not having any effect at all. Maybe because the air is dry. You sweat out alcohol in dry air.

'Sure. Go ahead.'

Want some?

'I had enough.'

I know, but do you *want* some?

'Shit.' He grips my arm like he is testing to see if I am really there. 'You are a smartarse.'

I'll get the bottle.

★

Theo has the same painting hanging over the bed in his cabin, the Japanese fishing boats, red in the sunset. He doesn't want me to talk.

His belt buckle comes from California, solid silver, beaten and drilled. His hands are big enough to pick me up, right off the ground. I didn't even dress properly, I've got my top and my jeans and he tugs them off and the only thing underneath is me, stretched out on the floor holding the wine bottle so it doesn't spill. I lie sideways on the floor, sideways in the dark, waiting. And he puts his hands under my head and cradles it like a grapefruit as he lifts me again, right off the ground like I weigh nothing at all, and the bed is narrow and the springs squeal and my hands reach up to the picture frame, spread on the sweating wallpaper and he asks what I want but I don't know, I say just more and he asks, like this, more of this, and I say yes, anything, just more and more and more of it.

★

The fan-heater stayed on all night. I open my mouth in the bathroom mirror. The back of my throat is raw from breathing.

'So it is…'

It *hurts*.

'Aww.'

His big arms go around me twice. Jesus. He can lift me – do you *mind?* – he can lift me off the floor.

'Gave you a sore throat. Are we still friends?'

Yes. I slept like a log.

'I noticed.'

I guess we missed out on the party.

'There'll be others.'

I bet there will.

'You should join us for lunch. The boys should be up about four. That's an early start for us.'

I think we're going this morning.

'Stay for the afternoon.'

She's – you taste funny – she's my lift.

'How'm I meant to taste?'

I dunno.

'You're going to town, right? You can get a lift with us.'

I'd... better not.

'Well, think about it.'

I came up with Babe...

'Okay. But you're welcome to. Okay? We're planning on staying in the city until our flight leaves. Some nice hotel.'

Where you can throw up on the carpet.

'Uh-huh.'

The cabin curtains billow out like skirts. Babe is reading in the morning sun, the blankets around her feet. The same picture hangs above her head. Junks in the sunset.

'Just something from work.' She flicks the pages. 'Not even interesting.'

I'm so tired.

'Was the party good?'

I sang.

'One of them came over and said hi.'

Oh.

'Some guy – Theo?'

I didn't know he came over.

'He said I shouldn't feel bad about what I did.'

That was nice of him.

'Nice. Sure.' She shrugs.

Do you want a glass of water? I'm going to have a glass of water. Jesus it's cold. What time is it?

'Come sit with me.'

I've got cramp.

'Slept crooked, huh?'

I don't know why it is. I look at the empty bottom of the cup. I hate drinking from plastic. I like a glass. Plastic does make water taste different. They did a test on it once. It's something to do with the oxygen bubbles that sit at the bottom of the cup when you fill it.

'Here. Sit.'

She examines my cheek, then my head. 'The swelling's down.'

It doesn't feel swollen at all.

'What was it like over there?'

It was a good party.

'Sounded it. Meet anyone?'

Lots of people.

She smooths the blankets.

'So what is it that I don't have to feel bad about?'

Pardon?

'Theo said I was forgiven, and I wondered: what was it exactly that I did?'

I don't know. You'd have to ask him.

'Did you say something to him?'

No. We talked about lots of things, but not about you. He's been all over Europe and the States.

'Trina.'

I said you were pissed off about the birthday not happening.

'The birthday was never *going* to happen.' She bristles. 'You lied about the party. Did you tell him that?'

I stand the plastic cup on the bench. You don't have to snap. It wasn't like that.

'What'd you tell him?'

You still had your birthday. Look, you're older. See? Without any help. My head hurts. I want to sleep.

'Didn't you sleep last night?'

What d'you care?

'With Theo?'

Maybe.

'What'd you tell him, Trina?'

Does it matter?

'Of course it matters. It matters to me. I'm your friend. At least I'm supposed to be. I don't feel like it sometimes. You drag me around. You bring me up here. You say everyone's coming and they aren't. You – you…' She throws up her hands. 'Last night!'

What about last night?

'I wonder what goes on in your head sometimes. I really fucking do.'

It doesn't matter.

'It does!'

I'm gonna go for a swim.

'You're not.'

I'm gonna get the key. Do you want to come? I feel like a swim.

'Trina I'm *talking* to you. I want to *talk* to you. I want *you* to *talk* to me.'

Is there a dry towel?

'What did you tell everyone about me?'

Nothing.

'What did you say?'

Babe stares. I can't find my towel. I look in my bag and underneath my bag and the bed. It takes forever to find. Maybe it isn't even worth going for a swim. You know how it is? You spend the whole night looking forward to something, and then when it comes to doing it, you don't want to.

Babe used to be a great swimmer, before. She took classes in it. Not that I went to classes. I wasn't going to be shouted at in front of everyone else. She showed me how at night, after the late class. I always forgot my towel. I remember having to go back into the changing rooms all the time. I left it at the gym and at home and at other people's places. In my locker. The smell of the changing rooms. Chlorine and piss and wet wood. My wet togs went mouldy. They squeaked on the bench as I sat down, squeezed out the water between my legs as I laid back with my eyes shut, waiting. The last locker doors banging shut with the lights off and waiting stretched out under the clothes hooks for the kisses and the stroking and the warm taste. Thinking, then, I don't want to go for a swim. Not just yet.

Theo swims, did I tell you? He has a stomach like a washboard, all the muscles. A real swimmer's body. He used to swim twenty lengths a day, a hangover from his college training. He was in a representative team. He could have gone for the Olympics, probably. He was that good. He shaved his body every day to cut down the drag and he clipped his hair short. But in the end he gave it up. He said he got sick of being in the water all the time, never lifting your head up. And I know what he means.

But there is nothing else to do. I have to go for a swim. It is either sit here and talk to you – her – or get into the water. And I like the water.

I shut the door behind me.

— EIGHTEEN —

The pool steam cools along the timber fence. There is a jet of hot water just below the surface, playing with my hands.

I don't let Babe in at first, when she knocks. I sit and hope she will go away. Explaining is such a waste of time. She knocks again. I reach out and undo the latch and the door opens.

She is still dressed. But the seats are wet, the ground is wet, the walls are wet. I mean, what's the point? Why don't you just get in? Why not? She talks about getting her togs. I mean... Jesus. She looks at me. She steps out of her skirt and piles her things in a heap and climbs slowly into the water.

The steam rises in curls. The curls do not last long. They thin and become invisible. Babe rocks from one side to the other, dipping her round shoulders in the water, carefully holding her hair so it doesn't get wet.

'I didn't want to do anything this weekend. I wanted to stay in bed.'

That's almost what you have done.

'I drove.'

Yeah.

She cups her nipple in the water.

'Are there pools for the other cabins?'

No. But they have nicer showers.

'How are the rooms?'

Bigger. Bigger and better.

She looks down like she understands. Her feet play with mine. I don't feel like it.

'Rub your back?'

It isn't dirty.

93

'Come on,' she says quietly. 'Turn around.'

I turn my back to her and she comes forward and begins to knead my shoulders, the muscles, the joints, cracking under her fingertips. She has strong, big hands.

'Everything's hatching out.' She wipes down by my spine. 'Being flushed.' My neck under her thumbs. 'Leaving your body.'

Everything aches. My legs ache, my tailbone. Do you feel a different part of you floating? With the baby?

'I hardly feel anything.'

Do you and Brian still do it?

She laughs. 'He's only just started speaking to me again.'

You can keep going until the eighth month.

'Can you?'

There was this woman who got pregnant for a second time when she did it in the ninth.

'Trina.'

I read it.

Babe smiles. She kneads my arms, the biceps, elbows, wrists. I didn't even know I had muscles there. I thought it was only bone. Gristle.

'What you said last night – about lying on the grass.'

Nothing.

'You said…'

I meant, your back lawn.

'At Dad's.' She recalls. 'It's sold now. Subdivided. It was the last big lawn in the street.'

It makes me smile.

'What happened after you left the pub on Thursday?'

Rub my stomach. She turns me round and runs her hand across my belly. Slow circles.

I tell her.

I tell her about the walk home, being angry. I tell her about swearing when my key sticks in the lock. About slamming the door and my feet slipping and my head. Calling 111 and not being able to speak. Have you ever lost your voice? You open your mouth and no sound comes out. The receiver waiting in the darkness. Eventually the operator decided on the police. I didn't call them. I thought I needed an ambulance. I thought my brains were dripping out of my head.

She stares at me with dark, dark eyes. The jet nozzle shimmers.

'Did you tell them?'

They were really stupid.

'Did you tell them what you told me now?'

No.

'What did you tell everyone last night – at the party?'

I didn't tell them I love you.

She holds her hands around my waist.

I lean forward and close my eyes and kiss her. She only offers her cheek.

★

Clean wind runs through the cabin. Everything is quiet and hung over. I could pack but I didn't bring anything. I run a comb through my hair so the water patters on the carpet. My head-cut has closed, nothing more than a pink line. I comb my hair over the scar.

The kitchen is dirty. The melon sits in the fridge with only one slice missing. The fruit is soft. When I move it from the bowl the mites float up. Ants stick in the juice. The fruit is at the extra-ripe, extra soft stage of its life, the last burst of sweetness before it turns rotten. We haven't even touched it.

I should leave a note but there's no pen and besides, Babe won't be surprised. She said she was going to do all the driving anyway. I will catch up with her later to explain. Maybe next weekend. Afterwards.

The manager watches me crossing the gravel carpark – he knows, the little prick. He probably peeks at the cabin windows. There was this guy once, in America, a serial killer who lived in a hotel. He used to trap his guests by…

Theo's cabin is empty.

All the cars have gone.

They said they were staying till four.

The next cabin is empty as well.

The beer cans are stuffed in a paper sack.

He said they were going to be there until four. He said come over for lunch. He was heavy on top. He put his arms round me and kissed me and lifted me off the floor.

The manager watches me walking back. He pushes the fly screen ajar and the dull metal squeaks.

'Left quarter of an hour ago,' he says.

He holds the fly screen open with one hand. It is a dirty screen, the aluminium flecked with white and grease and dirt.

Oh.

'I rang through their chit.' He holds the yellow paper. 'Credit card bounced.'

The yellow slip flutters in the wind. He turns it in his hand as if it's something he's caught and doesn't know what to do with.

He leans against the fly screen.

'Hmm.' He smiles. 'Did your other friends show up?'

I'm sorry?

'Your other booking. The one I forgot.'

I never booked. They're not coming. They never were.

'Really.' He raises an eyebrow. 'So you've lost them.'

The fly-screen squeaks shut behind him. Trucks are going by on the road. The sky is hard and blue with nothing in it.

— NINETEEN —

Babe is waiting in the cabin, sitting on the end of the bed, her cheeks red from the hot water. She has a towel wrapped around her. Her hair is stuck down in strands and the black elastic band she wears is tight around her wrist. She stands up when I enter. She wipes her cheeks. I scrape my boots on the mat and walk over to the sink and pour a glass of water and drink it slowly, in one gulp.

Babe lets the towel drop and stands barefoot on the carpet. I take her in my mouth and put my hand around the small of her back and guide her, stepping backwards to the bed. She undresses me, first my shirt and then my jeans. We fall naked into the bed, into the open sheets, and my mouth fills with her smell, her taste, my lipstick.

★

Sid Vicious and Nancy died after they OD'd together. When the police arrived the bodies were in a terrible condition. Normally it takes 24 hours before a body starts to rot, but Sid and Nancy started to rot straight away. The police said it was because they had taken so much heroin in the last few weeks. I think it was because they were so consumed by love that they were wasting away. All that killing themselves did was to get rid of the last thing that was left.

★

The curtains swell in the wind and the sunlight falls on the doormat. We left the door open the whole time. She laughs at that.

You would always pick fights with him. You were fighting when

I left, standing on the doorstep and screaming at each other. He was screaming at me as well but I didn't look back. He was telling you to keep out of it but you wouldn't. Telling you to keep out of something is as good as an invitation. Like a birthday card is as good as telling you to stay away.

You kept on shouting at him while I was loading my stuff in the taxi. The taxi driver was going to leave because he thought there was going to be violence. He didn't want to get involved or have to appear as a witness because that would mean losing work. He was telling me all this and trying to make excuses while I stuffed five dollar bills into his hand to stop him driving away with my things. When we got in the back seat you put your fingers through mine and squeezed.

My flat has nothing in it now. It used to be full of junk. Clothes and shoes and empty bottles. At night it feels as if everyone has booked out without paying, graduated and driven away.

Suddenly we are the only ones left, Babe and I. She is in the pool and I am standing on the verandah holding a baseball cap that isn't mine and the paper sack is full of bottles and the chit has bounced. The clouds are held low in the valley but we might as well still be sunbathing on her dad's lawn, or sitting at the end of the row at the pictures, or running out of the store, the doors opening at the command of the electric eye. I have sweated out the makeup but everything might as well be black and white and overdressed, I might as well be fifty or a millionaire and say that everyone did come up for the party after all. They should have come. They really missed something good. They probably wouldn't think it was something good – they'd probably be bored, and they'd say so. The others can be pretty cruel when they want to. They'd probably want to put a record on or change the channel or turn up the stereo until it thumped through the walls. But they did miss it, they missed something good, something amazing and rarely seen, like Marilyn Monroe's cunt in the newspaper photo – something you have to want to see before you can.

★

I could do a lot of things. I could clean up the mess in the room or make some phone calls or tell Detective Sergeant whoever or pick up the card and stand up and snap on the lights – I could do a lot of things. But not just yet. I don't feel like it just yet. I stand on the verandah for awhile, stand and listen to the trucks rumbling past, going back and forth, back and forth, back and forth, taking nothing nowhere and back again.

★

Babe is waiting in the cabin, sitting on the end of the bed. She is fully dressed. Her bag is by the door and her black leather coat lies across her knees. She stands up when I come in and wipes my cheeks. She goes to the sink and brings me a glass of water. She says, it's time to leave. I've had enough holiday. She picks up her bags. I drink the glass slowly, in one gulp, and stand it next to the empty bed.

— TWENTY —

'There are these two drunks driving home, Frank and Joe, and Joe says, Frank, Frank, we're getting closer to town. And Frank says, How can you tell? And Joe says: 'cause we're hitting more people.'

That's terrible.

Babe leans over the wheel, laughing.

That is terrible.

'Come on, it's a joke.'

And you a lawyer.

'Solicitor,' Babe says, wiping the tears from her eyes.

The wheels slide on the gravel road.

'So those guys bounced a cheque.' Babe shakes her head. 'That's classic. Truly. The manager hassles *us* for credit ID but when the boys come in he lets them through, doesn't check, doesn't worry – and he gets done. Seventy percent...' she raises her finger '...seventy percent of people committing credit fraud in this country are male. But it's the women they ask for ID. It makes you – what are you eating?'

I made Babe pack the fruit, in plastic bags.

'You don't have to eat it.' She makes a face. 'It's half rotten.'

It's only soft. Besides. It'd be a waste.

'It hardly cost anything.'

It's nice. Try some. I hold up a spoonful of melon and she takes it in her mouth like it's a dog turd, keeping her eyes on the road all the time. Come on. Chew.

She swallows. 'It should be fresh.'

It's not that bad. Fruit's good for you. You can tell when it's off because it goes rotten. You can tell just how fruit is and this is okay.

'I'm sorry. I'm scratchy.' She looks at herself in the rear view mirror. 'I feel awful.'

You look okay.

'It's because I'm tired. I feel like I was up all weekend. And when I do sleep I get woken up by your friend knocking on the door to tell me I don't have to be sorry for something I haven't done in the first place.'

He was only being nice.

'He was being a jerk. It's typical, you know? Typical fucking American. Him and all his piss-head friends being so up themselves that...'

Have some more melon.

'I don't want any more.'

Come on.

She looks worried, chewing. Take it easy, will you? I smooth her head. You frown. You're going to get an old lady's forehead.

'Hey: pay attention. I *am* an old lady.'

No you're not.

'I am.' She drums the steering column. 'And soon I'm going to be a lot older.'

She is going to do all these things she has never done before. And she will leave so much behind, everything, it will peel back like a shockwave.

'I'm worried about *what* I'm going to leave, you know? It's like having to move your entire house in one afternoon – I'm bound to forget the one thing I need, or leave something behind that's really important.'

You will take everything you need.

'And what about the other things?'

They'll follow.

'I hope so.'

They'll come running.

★

We pull over at one of the tourist places, a brown and white brick house done up with fake weatherboards and shuttered windows and a sign saying CAFE: MEAT PIES. She orders Devonshire teas while I sit by the window. Traffic runs past the wide glass, my reflection. The checkered tablecloth.

'Um! Cream!' She wipes her chin. 'The jam's fresh too. It's beautiful.'

After this the tea tastes bitter.

'I'll have yours if you don't.'

No. I'll save you from it.

The scones are warm and the cream is freshly whipped. Pressed between your tongue and the roof of your mouth it becomes liquid again. And it is nice. It tastes good.

'You don't get teas this good in the city.'

Oh come on.

'You don't. They're served in the hotels but they keep them a little too long.'

Conoisseur.

'Frances at work – you know Frances – she and I go out for tea once a week and it's never as good as this.'

Another logging truck goes past.

'They're stripping the forests out here. Clear-felling.' She crumples her napkin. 'When they're finished all the forests are gonna be gone.'

They'll grow back.

'Not the same forests, the originals.'

Close enough.

We watch the window. Across the road is nothing but trees – no buildings or houses. Only shade and a black mud gutter and pine needles six inches thick, the colour of rust. Underneath them is warm, where the bugs live – centipedes and ants, hiding from the birds.

Do you like your work?

'Not all the time. But mostly.'

What things?

'I like… working with other people. Helping them. A lot of people can't afford legal advice. They don't even know what's appropriate to them – their situation. We help them, and that feels good.'

Will you stay there?

'The pay's not good. But…' She tips her head. 'The harder things get for me, the more it makes me appreciate that… other people have it harder.'

You'll end up working for free.

'I think I practically do now. Besides,' She pats her stomach. '…I'm stopping in six months anyway.'

Will you go back to work?

'Not straight off. Brian'll be working, so…'

So who'll look after things when you do?

'Friends, I suppose.' She pours more tea. 'Are you volunteering for the roster?'

I didn't say that.

Babe holds her cup with two hands, smiling behind the faint traces of steam.

She lets me drive the rest of the way. I stomp on the accelerator, gobbling the miles between us and home, racing the trucks. Anyone would think we were in a hurry to get back.

★

The rain is waiting. Babe parks down the driveway so I can get out my things – and the fruit. 'Throw it out!' she urges. But it's fine, really, and I carry it to the steps and then go back and lean in the window to say goodbye.

'So this was my birthday party,' she smiles. Christ. I know. I'm sorry. 'It's okay.' She puts her hand on my neck. 'It was okay, it was fun.'

It wasn't fun really. It was a whole lot of noisy people in a hotel and a grumpy manager.

'Were you talking with him? Before we left? I saw…'

No. Not me.

'Oh.'

How're you feeling, your stomach…

'Good.'

I've made you late for work.

'I rang in sick.'

Did you? I can never do that by myself. I get a friend to do it for me. You know: hi, this is Catrina's flatmate and she's not feeling well…

'You should go flatting with someone again.'

I guess.

'You shouldn't be all by yourself.' Babe cups her breast, her nipple. And I put my hand on it lightly, feeling the swelling.

She looks up, red-eyed from the late nights and the talking and the drive and maybe something else and smiles and squeezes my hand. I lean back and fold my arms. She backs the car up the driveway, her long hair hanging out the window. I stand in the rain and watch her drive away.

★

The flat is so stuffy I have to open the windows. The lounge window has been repaired and the room smells of fresh putty. The new pane is a lot cleaner than the others. I guess I will have to clean them all, now. The police didn't clean up anything.

The people upstairs are banging around, arguing. I bet if I rang them up and complained – for a change – they'd still keep on doing it. They are arguing about tonight's dinner party: what to cook, who to invite. So it's going to get noisier but at least they'll stop shouting when their friends arrive. Because you never talk about anything with your friends – all you do is have a good time.

I feel like being by myself tonight. Here seems more peaceful than the motel, even though everything is still around you – the traffic and the buildings and the people upstairs. Being crowded isn't so bad. I like having things around me. I don't know what to do with the baseball cap. I put it on the bench for now.

The landlord came down, before. He's a neat sort of person. He's an architect. To build this place he collected junk from wreckers' yards and turned all the bits into something else and painted it white. Like the pillars by the door, they're not pillars at all – they're drainpipes, stood on one end. I'd like to build my house that way. Take the bits people don't want and turn it into something surprising. People appreciate your doing that, at least they do when you point it out to them. Most of the time they don't even notice.

The drive has really worn me out. I should eat something, but I don't.

I sit in bed watching the gas flames, the sheets around my chin.

★

My main concern is that it's not much of an ending. People used to say to me, Catrina, why do you say all this? And I could give them a hundred reasons, as many reasons as they like. I could even make some reasons up. But the real reason is simple. I like the endings. I can't be bothered with the little ones, myself. I like the big ones and the look on people's faces when they're over. I like everything to end in wide screen colour with the music swelling up and the audience cheering and the picture saying THE END.

The gas flames whistle. Night is outside, on the cold side of the glass.

The phone messages are still folded in my jacket pocket, squares of paper covered in the manager's scrawly writing. I put them on the floor by the bed. I will ring back tomorrow. Tomorrow first thing.

Good night from something-something city, something-something road. It's warm and it's dark. And there is no noise, and sleep is a nice place to be, but it could be better. You know? I could never have met Wayne and never left him. He could have just never existed. And Babe would never have met anyone else, either. She would have hundreds of clothes and shoes and change her look every day, like she used to. And she would be happier like that, she wouldn't be being sick in the mornings and worrying about her job and what's going to happen next, about forgetting things. I would really like to give you a story like that, really give it to you good, and at the end the camera would pull back to widescreen colour with the music swelling in your ears and the audience cheering and the last words would flash across the screen, THE END.

But in the meantime the gas flames burn soft, and paint the room blue, and that's the best I can manage. Even if it isn't, it will do for now.

Believe me.

— *THE END* —